CONTENTS

Murder Most Malicious in Malcesine

The Lake Garda Mysteries

Volume 2

K.T. ASHBOURNE

ISBN: 1723211389
ISBN-13:978-1723211386

DEDICATION

To Kim

ACKNOWLEDGMENTS

Thanks to the good people of Malcesine

1 WEEKEND AWAY

Svetlana sat listening to, and watching the proceedings of the meeting. Sara was quite nervous. She felt that she was under scrutiny. Svetlana gave away no clue as to how she felt, or what she was thinking. Sara droned on. Kim was dozing off.

"Kim!" yelled Svetlana suddenly. "Pay attention! This is important!"

Sara was delighted at this intervention, and could not help showing it in a broad grin.

Kim blushed, and sat up, attempting to appear interested.

Sara resumed her monologue. It was hot and close in the Ranch. Can't wait to get out and have a drink, thought Kim. She glanced at Alice and knew she wished for precisely the same.

A few minutes later, Kim could not suppress a yawn. It was really loud, and Sara halted in mid-sentence, fuming.

"Miss Tomlinson!" berated Svetlana "Do you mind? You're an uncouth slovenly wretch!"

"That's a bit steep, Svetlana" mumbled Griff, coming to her rescue.

"And it's Miss Kazinska to you!" snapped Svetlana.

Griff slumped deeper into his chair.

Svetlana turned towards Kim. "I have online access to the personnel system. I looked up your record. So tell me, why did you lie?"

"I didn't" Kim stated.

"You put down your next of kin as someone in Stretford, but we all know who you really are!" she riposted.

Griff sat up again, taking notice.

"Well, I thought it was best at the time" Kim mumbled.

"So. Lazy and liar" Svetlana concluded.

Griff glared at Kim. "Bloody liar" he concluded also.

Kim decided to say no more, she had dug her hole quite deep enough.

At last Sara uttered the words for which Kim had waited so long. "Meeting over!"

They all breathed a sigh of relief and relaxed. They each started to collect and organize their papers, and sort them into folders. Apart from Kim, who folded, and refolded them, then stuffed them in her purse. It bulged and groaned at the strain.

As they began to troop out, Svetlana spoke again.

"Miss Tomlinson, if you could spare me a precious minute of your time, I have some points I wish to make. This is not a request".

Kim winced, but Sara smirked with obvious pleasure.

Once they had all gone Svetlana's demeanour underwent a sea change, and she opened the conversation.

"Well?" she questioned.

"Well what?" answered Kim.

"What do you think about the weekend off? Didn't you notice that? I worked it so you have a Friday evening and then two days clear! Great, eh?" Svetlana beamed.

"Sorry, didn't catch that bit" she admitted.

"So you can do precisely what you like that weekend. You can sit in your room and sulk, get drunk at some crummy bar, eat chips all day, whatever you want" Svetlana suggested.

"Weekend off sounds great, thanks, Svetlana" and Kim smiled.

"I also have same weekend off. Lucky, eh?" Svetlana confided.

"Good. You deserve a break too!" Kim generously replied.

"Of course, I am not going to waste a single minute of it" and she waited for Kim's inevitable enquiry.

"So what are you going to do?" Kim asked on cue.

"I'm going to Milano, where there is a huge Pride Fest all that weekend. There will be a parade, and street parties, and open air concerts, it's going to be really huge" she enthused.

"Wow, sounds really great" Kim responded.

"So you want to come?" Svetlana airily hinted.

"Oh, I couldn't afford the cost" Kim retorted.

"Afford? Afford what? What cost? You will be my guest!" And Svetlana sat back and grinned at her.

"Oh, I'm not sure" Kim evaded.

Svetlana enlarged on her proposal.

"Look, I'm driving to Milano, you come along, no extra cost. I have already booked a hotel room, you share, no extra cost. You want to eat and drink, you pay for yourself, not that much extra cost. It will be fun!"

"Oh, I get it now. But can I think about it?" Kim asked hesitantly.

"Sure, think away, life is so long, plenty of opportunities arise every day, you just take your pick which ones you seize" Svetlana mocked.

"I will think about it, seriously" Kim promised.

*****

The next day Kim had a fairly easy duty. All she had to do was round up her charges, as per the list, from three different hotels, and then bus them on to Malcesine, a lovely little harbour and town, not too far from Garda. Only ninety or so minutes on the coach, so that would soon fly by. An easy stroll around the old town, with its incredibly quaint medieval streets, cobbled and barely three feet wide, a view of the crumbling castle, and then down to the pretty harbour for some lunch. She was really looking forward to it.

It all went to plan at first. The tourists enjoyed her informative and not too oppressive anecdotes of places of interest along the way. No refreshment stops were needed, so that helped too.

The coach ground to a halt, and parked at a peculiar angle, in the coach park, which must have sloped by thirty degrees.

She helped some of her elderly clients navigate themselves out of the steep vehicle.

"This is like abandoning the Titanic" one moaned.

Kim laughed. "You remember that, do you?"

They were eventually all out, and in good order.

"Let's see the castle first" Kim yelled, waving her Tomlinson umbrella high. "Follow me!"

They duly followed, and trod gingerly down the steep slippery streets. A flight of steps upwards to the right looked familiar, so she led them up. They struggled to match her pace, but once they had reached the summit of the flight of steps, they found they were all gathered together standing on the lawn of someone's back garden.

A middle aged native lady, about the size and shape of Griff's Fiat 500, emerged from her cottage and berated them roundly. She displayed a wide range of gesticulations and utilized a connoisseur's selection of expletives. While Kim had no doubt of their meaning, she held grave doubts as to whether any of the vocabulary thus employed could be found in any dictionary compiled by a Christian lexicographer. Kim apologized profusely to the irate native for the unwarranted intrusion.

"I know the way. I've been here before!" yelled an ancient man. He led them back down the steps, the crowd followed, and Kim brought up the rear.

The new leader led them on down the narrow lane. He regularly yelled to his brethren "Follow me, walk this way!"

The unfortunate man had a quite decided limp, and his unruly flock took him at his word, and began limping behind him. Kim laughed so much she had tears in her eyes as she witnessed this unlikely parade of geriatrics.

"Stop it, you naughty pensioners!" she pleaded repeatedly, but it was no use, they were having too much fun.

Their progress was halted by a yellow police tape closing off the lane. It was marshalled by a burly state policeman, who signalled them to return whence they came. Kim made her way to the front to see, but it was clear they could go no further this way.

"We'll have to go back up" she explained, so they all about faced, and slowly made their way back up to the coach park.

"We can find another way from there" she hopefully announced.

As they ascended the lane, Kim spotted the steps leading to the coach park. They all followed her up, to find not coaches but a well-armed middle aged lady wielding a broom in defence of her lawn. She advanced menacingly; they fled hurriedly, Kim uttered not one word of remorse.

Once they had secured the coach park, the ancient man again offered his services.

"I know another way" he boasted, "follow me, walk this way!"

So they did. Kim formed the rearguard to the whole platoon of volunteers, and once a true rhythm had been established, they hirpled in perfect synchronization down the street. Sorrowful natives made the sign of the cross as they saw this solemn column of misfortune hobble past, but were shocked to see their carer crying with mirth bringing up the rear, muttering to herself over and over "You naughty pensioners, you naughty pensioners".

They entered a small square, and looking down the length of a narrow street, could just see one tower of the castle, but access was once again prohibited by police tape and by no less than three guardian officers.

"Okay" said Kim, "we'll skip the castle and have an early lunch at the harbour".

There was no opposition to this suggestion, so they followed the lane down to the harbour, and dispersed among the little waterside cafés.

Kim ordered her latte, and then questioned an English speaking tourist at the adjacent table.

"Know what's happening at the castle?"

The tourist viewed her gravely. "They found a dead body early this morning. Looks like some climber tried his luck climbing up the castle walls. Fell to his death".

"Oh my God! That's terrible! Some silly tourist I suppose" Kim responded.

"Definitely not a local, they say. Must be a foreigner, stands to reason, the locals have more sense" her informant added.

"So they don't know who it was yet?" Kim wondered.

"State police are all over it. If they don't know yet, they'll soon find out".

"And there are signs all around the walls saying no climbing, aren't there?" Kim observed.

"Yes, but for some people that's just a challenge. They just want to show off to their friends" he guessed.

Kim's drink arrived, and she thanked the waiter, and her informant for the news. She looked around her, and noted that all her charges had now also gathered what had happened. It certainly dampened the mood of the outing, everyone who had minutes ago been so merry now looked quite sombre.

You never know the time or place, thought Kim, life can be so short. This resonated with what Svetlana had said, and she immediately resolved to accept her offer. What was there to fear? What was the worst that could happen? She was not obliged to do anything she didn't want, so why not go and see Milan and chance what may be. If some fat old lady propositioned her, she could tell her where to go in no uncertain way.

She reached for her phone, and called Svetlana. "Svetlana? Hi, it's Kim. Your offer for the weekend still good?"

"Oh, hi, of course it is!" Svetlana sounded pleased.

"Then I'd love to come! In fact can't wait!" Kim enthused.

"Brilliant! See you Friday six pm! Ciao!" and she was gone.

Kim glanced at her watch, decided to order some lunch, and sat back enjoying the sunshine.

*****

After lunch they slowly wound their way back up the steep lane, and finally arrived in the coach park. She counted them all on board, and signalled to the driver to set off. The coach growled as the gears were engaged and it crawled out of the coach park and back up onto the highway. Ever mindful, Kim swept up and down the aisle, recounting. She had one extra now. In a panic she recounted, checking each face carefully.

A scruffy looking young man in his twenties smiled at her.

"Who are you?" screeched Kim.

"Just need a lift to Garda" the youth grinned at her.

"Get off my coach!" snapped Kim, absolutely furious.

"Hey, chill, babe, just want a ride, that's all" the youth muttered, and then ignored her, and began regarding the view out of the window.

Kim marched to the driver, and asked him to stop.

"Not here. Bus stop" he answered.

The coach roared on for a mile or two, but then pulled up at a bus stop.

"Right, you, get off!" snarled Kim.

"No way, babe" he smirked.

Kim addressed the driver.

"We have a stowaway" she explained, "please eject him forthwith!"

The driver did not understand this, but rose to see what the problem was. He cursed roundly in Italian, and indicated to the youth that he should go. The youth did not budge.

"Look" said Kim. "A body was found this morning and right now you're the most likely suspect!"

That shifted him. He rapidly made his escape, to resounding jeers from the alarmed passengers.

"Sorry" said the driver. "Must have got on when I went for a break".

"No worries" smiled Kim. "Soon sorted him out" and she resumed her seat with some satisfaction.

*****

2 MILANO

Svetlana's Alfa Romeo swept into the hotel car park at an alarming pace as usual. Kim had taken good care to be behind a sturdy pillar, constructed she was sure, of ferro concrete, just in case. She need not have worried. The car halted with several inches to spare.

Kim crept out from her cover, smiled, and entered the proffered door. Before she could even say hello, the car lurched forward and screeched onto the main road. She attempted to buckle her seat belt, which is not easy when you're bouncing up and down over minor bumps in the road, and swaying left and right as the car is flung around every and any obstacle, both real and imaginary.

"Where did you learn to drive?" Kim dared to enquire.

"On a tractor on my uncle's farm" Svetlana admitted.

"Did many cows survive?" Kim asked timidly.

Svetlana roared with laughter. "Oh, I'm telling you, this weekend is going to be so much fun!" and she really hit the accelerator.

*****

The miles raced by, and so did the time. Once off the autostrada, Svetlana moderated her pace markedly, and drove into the city almost like a normal human being. She knew the way to the hotel, and the car was soon safely parked underground. Kim unbuckled her belt, stretched her arms, and staggered out of the car.

"Thanks for the lift, and the rollercoaster ride too" Kim managed.

"My pleasure. Okay. So now we see if room is ready as promised" Svetlana replied.

The receptionist assured that all was in order, and they shortly found themselves in a spacious and well-appointed room.

"Don't touch minibar, it's ridiculous" Svetlana cautioned, "we get plenty in outside bars".

"Could murder a latte" Kim replied.

"Okay. It's only ten. Let's party! We go out and find latte for you and gin for me!"

"Oh no!" yelped Kim.

"I joke. I need coffee too first" Svetlana admitted.

They ventured out immediately and quickly found a small bar, and had their drinks and ordered a few snacks too. Kim was astonished when the bill came.

"Wow! I knew Milano was expensive, but wow!" Kim exclaimed.

"I pay. No worries" Svetlana assured. She flashed her card and they were soon outside milling with the crowds. The streets were heaving, even at this time of night. A street stall beckoned, and they rummaged through the wares on offer. Kim bought a couple of postcards, Svetlana bought a T-shirt. They made their way to the main square, and were content to watch the merry throng for a while.

After a few more drinks, they returned to the hotel.

"I already checked room service menu. You have absolutely nothing to worry about, they don't serve chips and gravy" Svetlana quipped coyly.

Kim giggled. "Thank goodness for that".

As they were both tired out, they quickly showered and were soon in bed. Svetlana promptly fell asleep. Kim lay awake for a little while.

Must send a postcard to my mother, she mused.

'Dear mother, am in Milan having a wonderful time at the annual Pride Fest. Am sharing hotel room with maniac driving Polish lesbian more than twice my age. Wish you were here, love Kim'.

She laughed so loud she feared she would waken Svetlana.

She pictured her mother trying to slip grandad's wooden mallet in her handbag through the x-ray machine. She had always maintained that it would never show up.

She imagined her mother advancing with malice aforethought upon a hapless Svetlana, pleading innocence. With this unhappy thought in mind, she drifted off to sleep.

*****

Svetlana awoke first, and showered and dressed. She was sporting her new T-shirt.

It bore the legend 'I'm Gay – Try Me!'

Kim laughed. "You can't wear that!" she protested.

"But of course! It's so me. Suits me very well, yes?" and Svetlana twirled in it.

Kim laughed and went for her shower. She emerged in a very casual but modest outfit.

"That won't do, it won't do at all! How can you pull looking like you're on your way to the library to return overdue books? Boring!" and Svetlana flung something at her.

Kim opened the package to see an identical T-shirt.

"Oh, no!" she grimaced. "I'm not wearing this!"

"Of course you are! You want some fun, yes? Put it on straight away!" Svetlana insisted.

"I suppose" conceded Kim.

She quickly changed and viewed herself in the mirror. She blushed scarlet.

"Oh, you're so pretty when you blush" teased Svetlana.

*****

They found the breakfast room, and secured a table.

Svetlana had some fruit salad, some orange juice, and a coffee.

Kim had the same, followed by a continental breakfast of smoked cheese and cold meats, and a yogurt. Then she had an English breakfast, of sausages, bacon, eggs, mushrooms, tomatoes and beans. Then she had some toast. Then she had three croissants, one each with jam, marmalade and honey. More coffee, then some little cakes, and a few Danish pastries. She barely had any room left for a rum and chocolate truffle.

"That was so tasty" she announced at last.

"You don't have to eat your whole weekend's food all in one go" Svetlana advised. "There's no risk of a famine, you know. They're not running out of food".

"I was just a bit peckish" Kim explained.

"My God, and you're so thin – on this diet – it's amazing. If I ate like that, they'd need a wheelbarrow to move me around!" Svetlana cried.

*****

Once out in the bright sunshine, Svetlana took a selfie, and another, and yet another. She then insisted on a joint selfie. Kim objected. Her objections were swept aside. They posed side by side with a passing tram providing proof of location.

"I feel I'm going to regret this" Kim railed.

"Course not! Photo record is required! Always!" Svetlana asserted.

They slowly made their way to the main square again, picking up a leaflet outlining the various events of the weekend. They browsed at some stalls along the way. A DVD stall caught their eye, and they looked at what was on offer.

"This is one of my favourite movies" Svetlana stated, pointing to a DVD.

"Friends with Benefits, never heard of it" said Kim. "What's it about?"

"I can't tell you, it would ruin the movie" Svetlana riposted.

The parade did not start for two hours, so Kim suggested some conventional sightseeing. The cathedral beckoned, so they queued for tickets, and went in. The gloom and the quiet and the cool temperature inside made a deep impression on Kim. She enjoyed seeing the relics and sculptures, and artwork, but was glad to get back out into the sunshine and the merriment of the crowds.

"That's enough of that" concluded Svetlana. "Now I really want to see some queer folk".

Her wish came true soon enough.

An unruly clatter was heard in the distance, and a strange column of colour and sparkling motion crept into view. An attendant throng of travelling spectators kept post on either flank of the weirdest assemblage Kim had ever seen.

As the parade grew closer, Svetlana addressed Kim.

"See anyone you fancy?"

Kim regarded the scantily clad young men on one of the floats. Their trim figures boasted well developed muscles, and their flowing locks quivered in the gentle breeze.

"Sure do" admitted Kim. Pity they bat for the other side.

Some almost clad mermaids caught Svetlana's eye; she blew kisses.

"Make sure they see your T-shirt" Svetlana suggested, as she stepped onto a bench.

Kim laughed, and pulled her down.

They moved on to another area. Svetlana said 'ciao' to everyone they passed. Most replied, a few did not.

An old lady of at least seventy grabbed Kim's arm. "Love to, haven't time today" she said, indicating Kim's top.

The cheeky old dame vanished, leaving the two of them chortling with laughter.

They slipped into a bar for some lunch, which as it turned out, consisted almost entirely of prosecco. Svetlana displayed her social skills. She went up to each table in turn, announcing "I'm Svetlana, and I'm simply fabulous!"

Occasionally she was told to clear off, but generally she was welcomed, and had an extended conversation with her hosts. She also got a lot of drinks.

Kim watched in amazement. Svetlana periodically returned to her.

"Having fun?" she queried.

"Lots, thanks" admitted Kim.

"Why don't you talk to people?" she demanded to know.

"I just don't have as much confidence as you" Kim feebly uttered.

"No wonder you've no girlfriend. You're a wimp!"

"True" said Kim.

"Watch. I teach" and Svetlana returned to her task.

As evening approached, they ambled along to the square where the open air concert was beginning. It was so loud conversation was a practical impossibility. Kim was happy enough to listen and watch the show.

The moment it ended, Svetlana yelled "Club!" and yanked Kim down some streets and into a dark alley, where a ladies only club was located. Kim hesitated at the threshold, but was dragged into its interior. More loud music, but at least they could dance.

Kim danced for hours, with a bewildering variety of females swirling around her, it was a novel and intriguing experience. She did enjoy herself. More joint selfies were demanded and delivered. But, she wondered, could you really meet someone in a place like this, where conversation was effectively excluded?

It was a long and difficult stagger back to the hotel. They assisted each other in the task. Opening the door of the elevator was tricky too. So was remembering their room number. Several doors were tried before one opened at the behest of their key card. They took good aim at the bed, lurched forward and slumped upon it. Kim discovered that undressing is an arduous undertaking when you keep sliding onto the floor. Svetlana discovered that undressing was virtually impossible when your entire being is fully engaged in laughing at your roommate. They fell asleep in each other's arms, not so much in an embrace of romance, more that of a drunken stupor.

*****

Kim awoke to find Svetlana shaking her, and yelling "Breakfast!"

She needed little further encouragement. She might know nothing about picking up girls, but she did know how to select a good breakfast.

They went down to the restaurant, where Svetlana chose her regular modest victuals, and Kim decided on exactly the same as previously.

"I'm absolutely starving!" announced Kim.

This gave her ample licence to add a few little extras, just some additional cakes, and one or two more rum and chocolate truffles.

"These are so scrumptious!" she explained to a bewildered Svetlana.

"Where on earth do you put it all?" she asked in amazement.

"I'm a growing girl, you're all grown up" Kim observed.

"I'm only slightly older than you" she riposted.

"You know my age – nineteen - you've seen my file" Kim snapped. "I haven't a clue how ancient you are".

"I am thirty nine, for your information" Svetlana replied quietly, looking into Kim's eyes.

"That is more than twice my age!" Kim gleefully yelled. It did sound ancient when it was said out loud. "I knew it!"

"Not much I can do about it, is there? I keep trim and fit, and indulge in a very modest diet" she replied.

"Yup. Grant you that. You do" Kim admitted.

"So, fat girl, what shall we do today? There's more music in the square later, and stalls selling all sorts" Svetlana suggested.

"Well, skinny woman, that sounds fine to me" retorted Kim.

*****

They packed up everything from their room, checked out, and loaded the car.

"Later, we just drive off" Svetlana stated.

"Sounds like a plan. What time?" Kim asked.

"Six pm precisely" Svetlana answered.

They headed for the square again, and ambled around, checking out the stalls. Kim learned many new things, as Svetlana explained the various purposes of the myriad items on offer.

"I had no idea that I had led such a sheltered life" Kim ruefully observed.

"You're quite the little ingenue, aren't you?" Svetlana smirked.

"Suppose so" admitted Kim.

"I think I'll buy you a nice big present" Svetlana teased, holding aloft a huge sample.

"No! no! You mustn't!" and Kim blushed vermillion.

"You're so pretty when you blush" the unrelenting Svetlana replied.

The music flared, and Kim was saved. They spent the afternoon relaxing in the sun, and eating ice cream, as the bands played on.

*****

As the car cleared the outskirts of Milan, Svetlana posed a question.

"Had a good weekend?"

"Yes thanks, it's been brilliant. Best ever" Kim replied truthfully.

3 THE MAIN POINT

After the weekend away, there were a few normal days, where work dominated Kim's time, and no unusual occurrences presented themselves. Until Kim received a text from Svetlana, telling the team an urgent meeting would be held at the Ranch at seven pm. They all duly reported as directed.

Once all were seated around the table, Svetlana spoke.

"Thank you all for coming so promptly. Just one quick item. A new rep arrived in Verona, quite ill. She had to be taken to a doctor immediately, and he signed her off for a week, maybe two. So I need a volunteer to go to Verona to cover for one, maybe two weeks. Who is volunteering?" and she waited.

There was an eerie silence. No one said a thing. Kim looked at the others, and thought, well, if they're not volunteering it must be awful, so I'm not. Svetlana waited.

"I'm still waiting" she helpfully added.

The silence persisted.

"Okay. No volunteer, I choose" and she eyed each one menacingly.

"So, I choose new girl, lazy liar, good for nothing, two bit, daddy's girl, chalet girl, Kim!" and she pointed directly at Kim so that there could be no mistake.

"Strewth, Svetlana, that's a bit rough" Griff objected.

"And it's Miss Kazinska to you!" Svetlana blasted at him.

"So, Kim. Taxi at eight in morning. Empty room, everything out, pack your bags, ready to go at eight sharp. Maybe hotel make some money from their suite at last, eh?" she instructed.

"Okay, I've got it" Kim muttered.

"You poor sod" consoled Alice.

"Enjoy trips between hotels and airport, airport and hotels, and back and forth. Ad infinitum. Work all day, then all night, eat when you can, sleep when you can. Enjoy" Sara smirked.

"Hard cheese" Griff offered.

"We've all done it, your turn now" Rachel sympathized.

"I will cover three days of Kim's current roster, Friday to Sunday. You each cover one other day. Work that out among yourselves" Svetlana ruled.

"Meeting over!" decided Svetlana, and she strutted out.

*****

Kim guarded all her worldly possessions piled in a heap in the car park. The taxi was on time. The driver kindly loaded everything, and she climbed in with a heavy heart.

The taxi left the town, and headed up to the hills. Must be a short cut, no need to follow the bus route she guessed.

After half an hour, the cab halted. They were in a driveway, leading to a pleasant looking house. The driver got out, and began to unload her bags onto the drive.

"This isn't right! This isn't Verona!" yelled Kim.

Once all her luggage was assembled on the drive, he indicated she should get out. She did. He got in his taxi, and drove away.

The front door of the house opened.

"Miss Tomlinson, I presume" she heard. She peered to see who had spoken.

"Welcome to my home" said Commissario Sant Angelo warmly.

"Hi" managed Kim, completely surprised.

"Sorry for the subterfuge, but it was necessary. Do come in" and he grabbed her bags and led the speechless girl inside.

He set all the bags in a front room, then guided her to a rear lounge. It had a great view over the hills. The room itself was sparsely decorated.

"Do sit down, Kim" he invited.

"Thanks" she responded, and made herself comfortable. She looked at him anew. My God, she thought, he is so very handsome.

He smiled. "Sorry for the device, but this way only Miss Kazinska knows, you see, security, you know".

"Oh" said Kim. "I love your home, and this view is terrific. I like your sliding doors too. How does the mechanism work?"

She arose and fiddled with the door handles.

"You press the button, and lift simultaneously" he explained.

She tried, and the door opened. She slid it wide, and stepped out onto the patio.

"Wow! You can see the lake from out here! That's fabulous!" she exclaimed.

"I know" he said, "I live here".

"So if you extended out this way, just one storey, you could bring the view inside. Get it? You could reuse these doors too. Wouldn't cost that much. And reuse the patio paving stones. Anyone would do it. Easy" she added. She paced out the dimensions of the extension.

"You could have either a glass roof, or a tiled roof, depending on how much sun you want in. The choice is yours".

"Very kind of you, to give me a choice" the officer replied.

"No probs" Kim assured him. "And the new flooring could be ceramic tiles, no point in trying to match this out of date carpet that's dying on the floor before your very eyes" she helpfully advised.

"Can we get to the main point?" asked the policeman loudly.

"Right! Main point it is. The main point is that while your house is kind of okay, it could be so much better by adding a small extension. Just here" and she paced out the perimeter of the extension "and then this fabulous view would be yours all the time. Got it?" Kim summarized.

"Can I speak?" asked the patient commander.

"Of course you can" Kim assured him. "I love it when men speak up, and say what they're thinking. So many men just sit there, all dumb and brooding, and painfully reticent. It's great to finally meet a man who's willing to speak out plainly".

Kim paused for breath.

"Thank you, most gracious" he advanced. "So….."

"I've got to say I think your English is really good" she complimented.

"Thank you. And I think your English is reasonably good too" he quipped.

"Oi! You cheeky swine! You cheeky pig! I'll have you know I've got a GCSE in English language!" she boasted.

"That's impressive" he conceded, "but I've got a university degree in English, which is more impressive".

"Well bully for you, you big show off!" Kim laughed.

"Anyway, what I wanted to say……" but he was interrupted.

"I'm not usually so chatty. It's because I'm nervous. You make me nervous. Don't know why" she informed him.

"So, the main point……"

"I already covered the main point, and thoroughly at that" Kim interrupted again.

"The reason I invited you here…."

"I was wondering that very thing. It takes some explaining, too. Besides I'm supposed to be in Verona, we have a member of staff off ill. There's lots to do, not just sitting here chatting with you about improving your home. Talking of which, you need some pictures, the walls are really bare and need an uplift. As well as redecorating properly" and Kim pointed out the deficiencies and then stopped awaiting his response.

"Right. I'm calling the police. There's a woman in my home and she's talking me to death" and he reached for his phone.

Kim laughed heartily. "Sorry. I'll shut up now. Lips zipped shut" and she swept her fingers along her lips in simulation.

"The reason I invited you here," and he paused for effect, "was to ask you if you knew of anyone you could assist in the solution of a crime".

Kim nodded, but kept her lips sealed dramatically.

"A young man fell to his death in Malcesine……"

Kim interrupted once more. "Mmmm mmm mmmm mm mmm mm, mm mm?"

"Okay, you can speak" laughed the poor man.

She unzipped her lips with a grand gesture. "Yes, I know all about it, I was there that day. A climber tried his luck on the castle walls, but met his untimely end. Poor bloke. I was told all about it by some old codger in one of the harbour cafés".

"A young man fell to his death in Malcesine" repeated the Commissario, "or so it would seem. The body was found very early in the morning, and the state police arrived quickly and sealed off the area. Climbing ropes and equipment were found at the scene. Apparently he had fallen, and landed on his head, hitting a sturdy railing. His injury matched the railing, and there was blood on the railing".

"It sounds gruesome" said Kim.

"But one of the officers was not convinced. The blood splatter on the corpse was present, but it was not around the railing, but a little further out on the street cobbles. He called in the forensic squad, who examined the scene. A very detailed autopsy was also conducted. The Mountain Rescue Team was called to give their opinion. I have here the reports of the state police, the autopsy, the forensic squad, and the Rescue Team. So my sources are somewhat better than your source".

"I suppose so" admitted Kim.

"The Rescue Team said that the climbing ropes and equipment were all wrongly positioned for real climbing. They had just been placed there for effect. Further, there was no evidence that the wall had been touched, no pitons, or disturbance to the growing weeds, or surface dust. The forensic squad said he had been struck in the street, and the blood on the railing had been placed there for effect. The autopsy revealed he had been bludgeoned on the head, stabbed in the heart, and poisoned. The poison is not yet identified".

"Oh my God!" cried Kim. "That's horrific!"

"Yes, real hatred and malice in the slaying" concluded the policeman.

"A murder most malicious in Malcesine" echoed Kim.

"Exactly. Now he was not identified immediately, but as all his clothing and climbing gear was Australian, it did not take long to establish that he was one of a party of thirty Australians on an adventure holiday, staying in a hostel up in the hills, some miles away".

"An Australian? Awful long way to come and be slaughtered like that" Kim considered.

"This is true. The party was contacted, a role call was made, and one was missing. Their leader came and identified the body. His passport photo also matched the body. So we now know he was Steven Todd".

"Poor bloke" sympathized Kim.

"For the purposes of public record, we have given the impression that we have been convinced by the scene as set. So the culprit, or culprits think we have been duped. Now here is the real problem. The plane from Sydney landed in Roma, they got a coach directly to their hostel, and only met the hostel staff, who settled them in their rooms. Steven Todd did not survive to sleep even one night in his room, but was killed within twenty four hours of arriving in Italy".

"So the killer can't be Italian - the murder was premeditated - it must be one of the Australians!" Kim snapped.

"One, or two, or three of them" warned the officer.

He went on. "The state police interviewed every one of the twenty nine, as a matter of routine they explained, and obtained precious little information. No one knew him, and had hardly spoken to him. He was travelling alone within the party. Others had come with friends, in groups of two, three or four. Except the experienced leader, who is a regular every year".

"So he was a real loner, then?" Kim asked.

"Evidently. I was called in to help, in part because the crime was committed barely five hundred meters from my own barracks, so I consider it to be a personal insult, and I also interviewed them all, one by one, and learned nothing more".

"What about contacting the Australian police?" Kim suggested.

"Of course they have been informed of all the facts, and they have conducted a massive enquiry over the last week into the background and circumstances of every single one of the thirty. They can find no connection between the victim and any of the others. Steven Todd grew up and lived in a tiny town in central Australia. All the others, well, different towns, schools, colleges, jobs, industries, and so on. No contact via email or social media. The only discernible connection is this trip to Italy".

"And yet someone really hated him, it's like he was executed" Kim thought out loud.

"Our conclusion also. The case has gone cold. We have no more leads to follow. What we need is someone on the inside. Someone who doesn't look and sound like an Italian police officer. So can you recommend someone?" he queried.

"Well my colleague Rachel can speak Italian - she's fluent!" suggested Kim.

"These particular Australians happen to speak English – a language with which you have a passing familiarity" he ventured.

"Me?" Kim asked, ignoring the jibe.

"Yes, you. How would you like to be a secret police spy – a secret agent?" he smiled innocently.

"But what about my work in Verona?" objected Kim.

"There is no vacancy in Verona. I thought you understood this. That was just a cover story for your colleagues. So only Miss Kazinska actually knows you're helping us, but she does not know in what capacity" he explained.

"Oh. I finally get it. Bit slow there" she muttered.

"So can you help? You did so well alone in Limone" he tried.

"Of course! Right! Let's get cracking! What's the plan?" Kim asked as she bolted upright.

"Excellent! So. We have a two part plan. First, injection, second, monitoring" he elucidated.

"Okay. What's injection?" Kim asked directly.

"You can't just roll up to the hostel, and somehow talk your way into the group. No. The murderer would smell a rat. Wouldn't trust you. You'd get nothing. So. We make the injection their idea!" he gushed.

"Exactly how?" she questioned.

"We know they are going rock climbing this afternoon, and we know exactly where. All we have to do is have you dangling from a rope, stuck half way up the same cliff, and wait for them to come and rescue you. You will be a damsel in distress, and they knights in shining armour" and he smiled daintily.

"Dangling?" asked Kim, more than a little alarmed.

"Dangling, helplessly dangling" he merrily repeated.

"Not so sure about this plan of yours" Kim muttered.

"The Mountain Rescue Team will set it all up, and they will be on hand to actually rescue you if the Australians don't" he cheerfully added.

"So I just dangle there, for how long, do you suppose?" Kim justifiably enquired.

"No more than a couple of hours, max" he grinned.

"Then what, once I've been rescued?" Kim demanded to know.

"They take you in. Adopt you. Embrace you" and he demonstrated by making a hug.

"Okay. And monitoring?" she asked.

"Right. I have here a phone, looks normal, but is programmed to transmit continuous sound. We listen twenty four seven, record everything, and hopefully collect useful information. Also, any problem, we rush in and save you from the murderer, or murderers" he added reassuringly.

"I see. And how to I get any useful information?" Kim sarcastically enquired.

"No idea. Plan ran out there. You think on your feet" he postulated.

"Okay. Before I commit to this, I want a good lunch" Kim advised.

"Agreed. I make you sandwich and tea" and he laughed.

*****

"I carry camping gear and climbing gear, which is this pile. You change into these clothes, here, and you carry this bag. All you own bags stay right where you put them" instructed the Commissario, and he left her to change.

Once she was ready, they went out the front door. There was no car in sight.

"Only a short walk, your lift is around the corner" he explained, and they went up the road a few hundred yards and turned into a field.

"Are we going by tractor?" she jibed.

"Don't you always?" he enquired.

After a few minutes a beating sound was heard, which grew progressively louder. As it reached a crescendo, the Mountain Rescue helicopter came into view, and landed nearby.

"Your lift, madam" he indicated. The officer led Kim towards the machine, and the bags were loaded in. Kim scrambled in, and turned to assist the policeman. He backed away, and waved.

"Ciao!" he yelled, as Kim became airborne and flew away.

*****

4 INJECTION

The flight over the hills was a real treat, and as the mountains came into sight, the foothills directly below became much more rugged. The machine glided down to a gentle landing, and the team helped her out, and hauled out her baggage, and their own equipment.

The helicopter rapidly took off, and very soon all was silent. The team consisted of one woman and three men. The woman addressed Kim; she had a very thick Italian accent.

"Hi, I'm Anna, and this is my team. These two will quickly set up your tent and camp, over there I think" and she pointed, and two of them went off and did just that.

"Now, I don't want you to worry about a thing, we'll soon have you dangling helplessly half way down the cliff" she assured Kim.

"Oh" mumbled Kim.

"And if you need any help at all, just scream like a demented maniac. Okay?" she added cheerfully.

"Right. Wilco" Kim tried to sound as brave as possible.

"We'll have two up here, hidden, and two down there, also hidden. We watch everything good" she promised.

A man clipped a belt around her, attached a rope, and edged her towards the precipice. Kim had imagined a cliff of twenty or perhaps twenty five feet, suitable for amateurs. The chasm looming before her was hundreds of feet deep, and plunged vertically down into a darkened abyss.

"Just walk backwards, and you'll abseil down naturally" her guide informed.

Kim obeyed, and clumsily went down, her feet pressing firmly against the cliff face. Down and down she went, until the face, undercut by an overhang, was out of reach. She swung alarmingly on the rope, and was lowered from above, until she had descended sufficiently to commence her duty of dangling helplessly. Once she had got the hang of it, she felt she was quite good at it.

"I'm okay, dangling quite nicely" she called aloud for the benefit of her listeners.

The screen flashed on. 'Glad to hear it. CSA' it read, then the message faded away.

CSA. She laughed. At least Commissario Sant Angelo was actually listening.

She took in the view around her. She had to admit it was a fantastic view. So long as you didn't look down. In that direction, it wasn't so much fantastic as absolutely terrifying. She gazed into the distance below her, and spotted a column of people slowly crawling towards her.

They edged nearer and nearer, halting below her. Clearly they had spotted her too, and were pointing up to her. They removed their back packs, and a group donned equipment, and fastened ropes. Their upward ascent began, and she heard odd fragments of speech carried on the wind, and an occasional clanging sound.

Eventually one climbed to within earshot.

"Hey, you okay?" he yelled.

"Not really. Bit stuck" Kim yelled back.

"Hey, it's a Skinny Little Pommy Shelia!" he called into a radio.

"We'll have you sorted in a jiffy" he reassured her.

"Thanks, I'd appreciate that" she replied.

More of them ascended, and went above her, wishing her a g'day as they passed. She could hear a general commotion from the summit, then felt herself being hauled upwards. She turned to walk up the face, and was it was not long before she was scrambling over the lip and into the clutches of many arms.

"Oh, thank you all so much!" and she wept with relief, genuinely shaking from the experience.

"You dumb, or what?" demanded one of them, evidently their leader. "You never go climbing alone, and without the proper ropes, too! Crazy!" he scolded.

Kim smiled sweetly. "Sorry to be any trouble".

"This your kit?" he asked, pointing to her feeble tent and pitiful camp.

"Yes" she admitted.

"Well it's crap" he scorned. "Utter rubbish! You'd better come down with us. Join our party if only temporarily".

She agreed, as did the others.

The remainder of the party ascended the cliff, and they all made merry on the summit. Many photos were taken.

"Hey, SLPS, come and have a selfie with your saviours" one of them yelled at her. She obliged, and smiled sweetly.

The leader accosted her once more. "Sorry about yelling at you before. My name's Hank, group leader. You know, I wasn't kidding about climbing alone. We just had a fatality ourselves. First night one of the guys got the dumb idea of scaling the local castle walls. He fell and died. Just like that. We didn't even get to know him at all, he was gone".

"My God, that's shocking!" Kim exclaimed.

"Yeah. It's been a real downer. And we lost two days to police interrogation, they asked us all loads of dumb questions".

"I bet everyone's pretty depressed after that" Kim ventured.

"Too true. In fact rescuing you has cheered everyone up, taken our minds off all that crap" he reckoned.

"Glad to be of service" Kim quipped.

"Okay, you're okay. So let's all get down, but properly this time" Hank suggested.

They assembled once again, and packed up Kim's camp for her, and were soon all making their way back down. This time Kim felt quite relaxed in their care.

Once all were safely down, the troop repacked everything

and moved out, heading back to the road and their coach, and the drive back to their hostel.

The hostel swung into view, it was really quite posh thought Kim, she'd been expecting a real dive. Once all was unloaded, Hank said "Wait here" to Kim, and went inside to consult the Italian hosts. He reappeared shortly.

"So, SLPS, the man says the bunk is paid for, the tucker is paid for, the activities are paid for, so if you don't mind stepping into a dead man's shoes, you can have his holiday, or what's left of it. You game?"

"You bet! Wow! That would be great! Is it okay with everyone else? I don't want to gatecrash" Kim enthused.

"I think they'll be proper chuffed" he said.

Kim was shown to room twenty three, which was clean and empty.

"Police cleared it" Hank advised. "Ship shape now. Tucker at eight, common room" he invited.

"Brilliant!" responded Kim, settling into her new accommodation.

*****

At eight o'clock Kim entered the common room, which served as the canteen. Benches and tables were lined out. The room was clean, but not well appointed. Seen worse, thought Kim.

A huge cheer erupted when they all saw her. She smiled nicely.

"Thanks everybody for saving me" she announced in a squeaky voice.

"No worries, SLPS" was the general reply.

She made a further announcement. "My name is Kim".

"No worries, SLPS" many replied.

"Lovely name, SLPS" others added.

"What's SLPS?" she enquired of the young man next to her, once she was sitting down again.

"Skinny Little Pommy Sheila" he explained.

Kim laughed. "That's horrid! My name is Kim".

"Cheers, SLPS" he said, sipping at his beer.

Kim looked around at the gathering. Twenty nine doesn't sound a lot, but it seemed to be a sea of faces to her right now. And one or more must be a killer. And they all looked so nice.

She chatted easily with them, while they all ate, Australians are so much fun she realized. And they all seemed to be in such a cheerful mood.

Later Hank approached her. "Tucker okay?"

"Yes. What it lacks in quality is compensated for in the sheer quantity" she replied.

"We need to eat well. Busy day tomorrow. Canoeing on the big lake. Anyway, you tucked in too" he observed.

"Well, I was starving" she replied.

"You up for canoeing?" he asked.

"You bet" said Kim.

"Experienced or novice?" he demanded.

"Novice, novice at everything" she coyly smiled.

"Oh, you're gonna be so much trouble!" he groaned.

*****

At night in her room, she said out loud 'so far so good, night everyone' and glanced at her mobile.

The screen glowed briefly 'Si, buona notte'.

She then put it on charge, and switched it off.

*****

The ancient coach sounded like it was grinding its way through at least half a dozen gearboxes. It produced an ungodly screech and an unpleasant aroma of burnt brake linings as it bumped to a halt on a grass verge by the lakeside. A large hut was nearby, and strewn around it were canoes, paddles, lifejackets and helmets. The water's edge was just a few yards away. The happy assembly disgorged from the bus.

Hank yelled at them.

"Right! Experienced canoeists assemble on my right, and all the novices to my left".

He indicated the directions for those unsure.

"Experienced – here – novices – here".

Kim strolled to his left. Everyone else huddled on his right.

"Right! Experienced ones, get your gear on, get going, no going alone, you know the drill. Lots of places up and down the lake to get lunch. Back here for four thirty sharp. No exceeding the lake speed limit of sixty miles an hour. Keep clear of the ferries, they have right of way. Anyone thinking of drowning, call me on your mobile first to see if it's okay. Got it? Any questions? Right. Get going!"

All the others jeered as they left. "Novice, novice, spot the novice! She's more of an expert in mountaineering!"

He turned to his left to face the novices.

"Right. Novices. Form up in good order, and step closer so you can all hear me. Right. Let's count you all. One", and he looked around, "one, one" he repeated, recounting Kim, "one, looks like we've just got the one then".

Kim curled up laughing.

"Sorry about this, I'm ruining it all" she cried.

"Not at all. I was a novice once. So were all that lot. It's important to learn these activities properly, have the proper training and equipment. That stunt you pulled up in the hills was bordering suicidal. If the Mountain Rescue Team had seen you, they'd have arrested you. They're attached to the police in Italy, you know".

"Oh. I didn't know that" she admitted.

"So, I'll show you the gear".

Hank went through all the details of the gear, its design and safe operation. Kim listened attentively. She glanced occasionally at the others, most already far out on the water. Two were holding back, paddling close by.

They slipped their vessels into the water, and Kim was afloat. She followed all the instructions, and was soon paddling erratically, but she was definitely paddling.

"Thought we'd keep you company Hank, in case you get fed up with the SLPS" one of the tardy two cried.

"Cheers mates. Hey, SLPS, this is Tom, and this is Tim. Confusing, eh? They even look alike. Tom's the ugly one, and Tim's the even uglier one" Hank explained.

"Hello" Kim sweetly greeted them.

Tom took up station by Kim's left, and Tim by her right. They paddled slowly along. Hank seized the opportunity to show off, and sped away.

"So, where are you both from?" Kim enquired.

"Australia" they answered in unison.

"Whereabouts in that tiny island?" Kim insisted.

"Perth" said Tim.

"Adelaide" said Tom.

"So you're not from the same place - you seem to be such good friends" Kim observed.

"Cousins" they answered in unison.

"More like brothers, really" added Tom.

"Yeah, he's like a brother, but I'm more like a cousin" Tim corrected.

Kim laughed. Well these two didn't seem like murderers, that's for sure. They chatted amiably until Hank returned.

"Getting the hang of it?" he asked.

"Yes, it's great" Kim replied.

"Right. An hour or so that way is the pretty little town of Limone. Let's aim for it, and get some lunch there. Nice and steady now" Hank suggested.

"Super!" cried Kim, and they paddled away in a little flotilla. What a fabulous way to travel, thought Kim. No noise, or hustle or bustle, incredibly tranquil and beautiful gliding across the lake.

*****

Kim sat in the pretty little main square of Limone with her new companions. It really was wonderful just sitting there, enjoying a delicious lunch, soaking up the sun, sipping a fruit juice - no booze allowed when on the water Hank had cautioned - and not having to scurry around looking for a dead body. So glad I didn't say that aloud, Kim mused. This is definitely the life, she concluded.

*****

In the evening they all gathered in the common room of the hostel. A large supply of hamburgers and chips was on offer, an offer which was gratefully accepted by all. Kim managed to eat more than the three others on her table.

"Well played, very nicely done!" congratulated one named Pete.

"Yeah, I've never been able to down four burgers in one go. Sound" chirped Sam.

"Greedy SLPS if you ask me" ventured Slugger. Kim could not imagine that Slugger was his given name.

"Thanks. I was absolutely starving" Kim responded.

"So how come you're not as fat as a brick shithouse?" queried Pete.

Kim could not answer for laughing.

"Yeah. All the sheilas I know that scoff like that are as fat as brick shithouses. You need a fork lift to get them on their backs" informed Slugger.

"Yeah, and you need a crowbar to prize their knickers down" added Pete.

"Still give 'em one though, eh?" interjected Sam.

"Too true, mate" the other two chimed.

"Really!" managed Kim, "Such vulgar talk when a lady is present".

"Where? Where?" and they all looked around in an exaggerated fashion.

"I am accustomed to an after dinner repartee that is more delicate and refined" Kim objected daintily.

"Don't mind them. They're from Burra Burra. In Burra Burra they think repartee is a special way of cooking cabbages" explained Sam.

The conversation continued in this vein until late.

Hank arose, and banged his table, to make a brief address.

"SLPS and gentlemen, your attention please. A novice has completed canoe training today, so when your name is called, please come up and collect your certificate" he announced grandly.

"SLPS"

Kim advanced to the front, and accepted the certificate graciously, to a blend of applause and jeers. She curtseyed dramatically and repeatedly. She returned to her seat and read the document.

It read 'Certificate in Canoeing Competence' in bold on the top line. The name entered on the second line was 'Skinny Little Pommy Sheila'. A document to treasure, she resolved.

5 MONITORING

The next day's activity was caving. Kim imagined a large spacious cavern, with electric lighting and carefully installed concrete steps flanked by sturdy hand rails, with regular elegant notices pointing the way out. And indeed so it was for the first two hundred metres along, and fifty metres down. Carefully lit signs informed you just so. A steel barred gate sealed off the entrance to the unsafe areas. You knew this because a sign on the gate read 'Unsafe beyond this gate' in both English and Italian.

They reached the foot of the concrete stairway.

"Well, that wasn't so bad, after all" Kim said in a ponderous whisper, but it reverberated all around and echoed peevishly.

A ripple of derisive laughter greeted her comment.

"Right!" yelled Hank. The echoes made it sound there were at least a dozen of him. He pulled out a bunch of keys, and freed the gate.

"Right! Let's get started then. You two stick with the SLPS, and off we go!" and he led the way in.

Helmet lamps flashed on, and they marched down a steep

slope, and as the walls narrowed, formed a single file, and as the roof lowered, slowed to a shuffling crouch. Kim clung to her escorts for dear life. They entered a tiny cavern, and all squashed into it.

"Right!" yelled Hank. "This is base one. Three ways onward, this way hard, this one harder, and this one bloody hardest of all".

He helpfully indicated each with his torch.

"Novices with me the hard way. Everyone else, take your pick. Everyone write your name on each way list, and then everyone gets a copy of every list so everyone knows where everyone else is. Got it?" he directed.

This feat took several minutes to accomplish.

Kim and her two escorts, together with Hank, were the only ones going the hard way. Evidently all the others were too tough to be seen going an easier way with a mere girl.

The four set off the hard way. Hard meant sliding out of the tiny cavern through a tight crack, and slithering along it, until its roof raised sufficiently so that a steady rhythmic crawl could be employed. An upward curve forced a leg jamming vertical climb, followed by a sickening lurch downwards courtesy of a steep slope, which ended on a narrow ledge overlooking an ebony precipice.

"Stay on the ledge, don't plunge over the precipice" Hank cheerfully advised.

"Creep leftwards, keep going, and it opens out nicely into a charming picnic area" he encouraged, "but mind not to plunge over the precipice".

They were gracious enough to heed his directions, and

assembled in a white cavern, featuring spectacular stalactites and stalagmites.

'Now this really is something' thought Kim. She took a couple of pictures.

"This is fabulous!" shouted Kim, and it repeated for some time.

"No need to shout" suggested an escort.

"I'm Alexander, by the way, Sandy for short" he introduced himself.

"And I'm Alexander, Alex for short" announced the other.

"And I'm Kim" she replied. "Great to meet you both".

"Likewise" they chirped.

"So where are you two from?" Kim enquired.

"Brisbane" answered Sandy.

"Gold Coast" replied Alex.

"Gold Coast! That sounds so exotic!" exclaimed Kim.

"Yeah, it really is. Even the street lamps are made out of pure gold, they're so bright and shiny at night" he explained.

"Oh, right, I must visit sometime. Bring a chisel and hacksaw along" Kim retorted.

"Hey, self-confessed vandal here Hank. Straight up" Sandy jibed.

"Talking of which, don't touch any of the formations, they're delicate, and have taken thousands of years to grow. Leave them for future generations to appreciate" Hank informed them.

Kim regarded the natural sculptures anew. She was glad to have access that was denied to the general public.

"Right" said Hank. "Time to move on to the dainty little Angel's Grotto. Everyone game?"

They all assented.

"First, we all need a quick refreshment, drink a little, and a tiny snack" he directed.

They sipped from water bottles. Kim got her sandwiches out.

"Too much" advised Hank.

She put one sandwich away.

"Still too much" he repeated.

She put half away.

"And again" Hank insisted.

She tore it, and put half back. "This is barely a mouthful" she moaned.

"Just right" Hank grinned. "Now, see that dark corner down there? We empty our bladders there, because onwards is a tad tight".

Kim hesitated. The three men quickly achieved their task.

"You next" Alex invited.

"I will do no such thing!" Kim railed.

"It's here or later into your panties. Choice is yours" Hank helpfully informed her. "We'll turn our backs".

They solemnly rotated. Kim advanced and scrambled into the void, and filled it as best she could. She resettled her clothing, and turned to see the three bright faces grinning at her.

"You pigs!" she yelped, and they laughed heartily.

They slithered along, hoisted themselves up, slipped down, curled around, and crawled into a quaint little cavern featuring a formation, which when viewed from a very specific angle, was nothing like an angel.

"Is that it?" fumed Kim.

"It's more a figure of speech, to encourage the timid" explained Hank.

"Nice grotto though" observed Alex.

"Yeah. It's a real belter" opined Sandy.

"Reminds me of my grandad's shed" Kim ruefully sighed.

"People would kill to see this. Once in a lifetime experience" Alex mused.

"Too true mate" Sandy added.

Hank addressed Kim, and seriously for once. "You know, Kim, I'm so glad that you stepped up and joined this holiday. It's changed the whole mood. I mean, before everyone was so down following the fatal accident, and we lost two days of activities to police interrogation. Now, all that's been forgotten. You haven't half lifted up everyone's spirits. Good on you".

"Yeah, well done" the others agreed.

"Everybody happy?" asked Hank.

"Never better" replied Kim, taking a photo of the hidden treasure, from a very specific angle.

*****

6 ELIMINATION

Back in her room that night, having showered, changed and dined, all twice, Kim was combing her hair, regarding her reflection in the mirror.

"You brave girl!" she cried aloud.

Her phone glowed. She read the message 'We think so too' before it faded away.

"Did you get all that down in the caverns?" she enquired.

'Picked up the recorded feed when you resurfaced' it glowed.

"I'm not sure I'm doing any good here" Kim suggested. "Don't seem to be getting anywhere".

'You're doing fine. Gaining everyone's trust. Just keep going. CSA' was the response.

"Okay. Anyway, goodnight!" she called.

'Buona notte' it flashed before she switched it off and went to sleep.

*****

"Right!" yelled Hank. "Welcome to Asiago Airport! Skydiving! Doesn't matter if you've done it before or not, everyone's considered a novice, and we spend the morning training, and then jump in the afternoon. Luigi here is your trainer, You do everything he says, or you don't jump. Say 'hi' to Luigi".

"Hi to Luigi" they all obeyed.

They spent the morning leaping off progressively higher benches, rolling on floor mats, gliding down cable slides, and fiddling about with ripcords, helmets and goggles. Kim was faint with hunger by lunchtime.

"Right" said Hank. "Everyone's passed, so everyone can jump. Time for some quick nosh, then check your flight times on the list posted there" and he indicated where. "Any questions?"

Kim timidly raised a hand.

"Yes, SLPS?" Hank invited.

"What if the plane crashes into a mountain?" Kim asked.

"No worries at all. We're fully insured, and in the event of a blazing crash, any compensation due, payable to the region of Veneto, for damage to the mountain, will be paid by the insurer. The executors of your estate won't have to pay a penny. Better still, no funeral costs for your family, because the remains of your body will be scattered over a wide area, nourishing the local fauna and flora. Very ecological. So no worries at all" Hank reassured. "Lunch this way".

Kim saw the salami pizza, and thought I could devour that with a vengeance, which she did, and then swilled it down a tin mug full of cheap lager. And now I could really murder a decent cup of tea, she thought to herself.

Kim sat anxiously with her squad, awaiting their turn. The first few had already landed, and the second group were now embarking.

"I'm Kim" she said, introducing herself.

"Tony" "Phil" "Bodger" "Iqbal" "Ahmed" they responded.

"So, Bodger, what was your mother thinking when she christened you 'Bodger', I wonder?" she asked.

"She's a religious nut. Named me after Saint Bodger The Beneficial" he replied.

"Indeed? And who, pray, were the fortunate recipients of his blessed beneficence?" Kim enquired serenely.

"All the maidens of the district, both fair and foul. He'd give 'em all a good rogering and then marry them off to the local peasants" Bodger enlarged.

Kim roared with laughter.

"I do my best to follow his example" Bodger added.

"He does too" supported Tony.

"Sometimes fails, falls by the wayside. Some sheila says no, then he has to do his penance, pray for forgiveness for two days" added Phil.

"Well you're not marrying me off to some local peasant, so you can forget the other" Kim riposted.

"Two days penance right there, mate" said Tony.

"I seek solace in the inspired life of my patron saint" Bodger wailed.

"We have no saints of this type" stated Ahmed emphatically.

"No. Only mullahs" added Iqbal.

The plane taxied in, and their moment of doom was upon them.

It was so noisy in the cramped little plane, conversation was a chore to be avoided. The machine crawled up to its designated height, and a lamp flashed on. The engine quietened, two went out, and Kim advanced to the door and in a flash was hurtling earthwards.

She gazed around at the view. The lake was obvious, and so was Verona, clear as a bell. In the distance she could see the coast, the lagoon, and Venice itself.

She yanked the ripcord, and slowed dramatically as her parachute unfurled. It was a delightful swaying motion, drifting down gently, and then an abrupt thump as solid ground was underfoot.

All praise to St Bodger The Beneficial, she thought, as she realized she was still alive.

*****

During the evening meal, Kim sat with some new comrades.

"I'm Kim. I'm the girl" she added helpfully.

"We hadn't noticed" one replied. "You eat like an Aussie, and smell like one two" he remarked.

"Don't be so revolting!" objected Kim. "I have a refined feminine aroma, quite unlike the stench you lot reek of".

They laughed.

"Good to meet you, I'm Roger, so you know where to come if you need a good....."

"Ignore him. He's just all talk. I'm Mike, by the way" and he smiled.

Kim looked at him anew. He was really handsome.

"Hi, I'm Big Richard, but you can call me Big....."

"But you don't have to if you don't want to" interrupted Roger.

This banter continued throughout the meal, after which they all separated into different conversational groups.

Sitting alone, Kim felt quite elated. Yesterday had been exhausting, but today had been a great day, without too much strain.

So, she thought, what is a fair maiden to do in a hostel full of twenty nine hyperactive testosterone drenched young men? Make hay while the sun shines, she concluded.

She decided she might quite like some beneficence herself.

Once more she reconnoitered her herd of prey through the eyes of a predator.

She selected her quarry, and smiled at him, directly and constantly - her favourite come hither smile. The youth came hither.

"You okay there?" asked Mike.

"I am at the moment. But I was just thinking, I'm twenty three, and I'm in room twenty three, and at twenty three hundred hours I get desperately lonely" she simpered.

"Is that right?" he responded, his interest piqued.

"It is right," she assured him, "but it's wrong. Is that a wrong you can right?"

"Oh yeah, sure can" he claimed.

"Tap gently on the door three times, then once more, then once more, twice strongly, and once gently" she instructed.

"That like a signal?" he queried.

"Morse code" she said.

"What's it say?" he was dying to know.

"S E X" she explained.

He nearly fainted. "I'll be there" he promised.

"Don't be late, and don't come early either. Bring protection" she warned.

*****

At the set hour, Kim switched off her phone, and as soon as she heard the taps, flung the door open. Mike slipped through the doorway, and they immediately kissed.

She began removing his shirt rapidly, revealing an extensive array of tanned muscles. He reciprocated the gesture, and caressed and kissed her breasts. She moaned with pleasure.

He swept her off her feet, and gently lay her on her own bed. She soon succumbed to his advances, and yelped "Mike, overcoat!" just in time. He did what he needed, then did what he needed.

Kim orgasmed loudly, but then so did he. He filled two more overcoats before he was finished, and while she only came the once, she relished the efforts employed.

They lay there, gasping.

"That was so good, Mike," Kim affirmed, "so good".

"Too true, too true" he contributed.

They lay awhile basking in the heat of the moment.

"Mike, you'd better head off now" Kim suggested.

"You sure? Not lonely anymore?" he asked.

"All cured" whispered Kim.

He dressed, blew a kiss, and sloped off.

"Now that was satisfactory", said Kim aloud as she dozed off to sleep, "most satisfactory".

*****

7 WATERSPORTS

The coach lurched and swayed its way up an ever steepening incline, and flung them all first to the left, and then to the right, as it hurtled around hairpin bends, horn blaring. In places the coach was wider than the road, and it ran over a few roadside rocks for good measure, the better to enhance the experience. Periodically a plunging drop would form the verge of the road, and those lucky enough to be in window seats could relish the vertical view down into the abyssal depths. But all good things come to an end, the coach stalled and slowed to a halt, and they all reluctantly disgorged into a broadly horizontal mire.

"Right!" yelled Hank. "Swimming! Just a couple of miles on foot up to the pool. Who's ready for ten lengths?"

"Yey!" they all responded.

"How about you, SLPS?" Hank pointed directly at her.

"I'm good for ten lengths" she assured him.

"Right! Off we go!" and he led them straight up the steepest part of the incline at a brisk pace.

Two miles may not sound like all that much, but up such a steep slope, and at such a rush, it was a real effort for Kim to keep up.

They cleared a grassy summit, and the pool came into view. It's clear blue waters reflected the nearby rocks and surrounding mountains, it was truly picturesque.

Kim stared, and took in the view.

"Right!" said Hank. "Shallow end here, deep end there" and he indicated the same for those who had not understood.

"Pool is seven hundred and fifty metres long, so ten lengths is seven thousand five hundred metres. Get cracking!" Hank instructed.

They began disrobing, and plunged into the virtually freezing water. A column of swimmers was soon making steady progress towards the centre of the pool.

He approached Kim. "Look, realistically, I don't think you're up for this one".

Kim stared aghast at the sheer size of the lake.

"I don't think I can manage a tenth of a length, never mind ten whole ones" she timidly admitted.

"Okay. You comfortable swimming just here in this shallow zone?" Hank suggested.

"Yes, that'll be fine" Kim gratefully accepted the suggestion.

"So this is your comfort zone?" Hank asked.

"Yes" Kim replied.

"Well, I don't want you to remain in your comfort zone. You've got to challenge yourself. How about you swim once around the perimeter, keeping close to the shore, so you can easily slip out?" he indicated the shoreline all around for the purposes of clarity.

"Okay, I'll do that then" Kim accepted the challenge.

"We'll keep an eye on you" he promised.

Hank was soon in the water, making up for lost time.

Kim disrobed, revealing the swimsuit the police had kindly packed. Her trim figure crept into the water. Her trim figure rapidly exited the water.

"Bloody freezing!" she yelped.

She drew twenty deep breaths, braced herself, and plunged into the icy ripples.

She managed to get a quarter of the way around the perimeter, then retreated to her comfort zone, decided that was not so comfortable after all, and slipped out onto dry land.

The sun was rising higher, and as she sat on a flat rock, realized it was quite warm. She found a larger, flatter rock, and resolved that the best use of her time would be to top up her tan. After fifteen minutes she was quite dry, feeling very proud of her achievements, and entirely happy to watch the others thundering up and down the lake.

Her mind turned to the question of the task she was undertaking. All the activities were great fun, but she was no nearer to resolving the puzzle. Her phone was close by.

"What was the name of the small town Steven Todd came

from?" she asked aloud.

The screen glowed. 'Katherine, Northern Territory'.

"What's the population?" she demanded.

'Wait' it glowed, and faded.

"6300' was the message that followed.

"Thanks for that" Kim muttered.

She stretched out in the sun, and ruminated over all she knew. Guy from a small town. Very small, way out in the middle of nowhere. He books an adventure holiday – quite understandable. Then is slaughtered within hours of arrival. Not just slaughtered, executed. It was preplanned. He didn't know his killer, or killers, or he'd have run for it, or raised the alarm upon seeing them. But they knew him. And were determined. And all these men seem so nice, in fact they are nice. No bloodthirsty thugs here, she thought.

Some words she herself had spoken drifted into her mind. Right a wrong, vengeance, murder.

She had it. This was a preplanned vengeance killing, for some wrong done in Australia. And they couldn't exact revenge in such a small town, they would have stood out. They waited until he left his safe haven, then struck as soon as possible. And the original wrong done had not been to him, the killer, or, them, the killers, but to someone else. A friend, or more likely, a family member, had been Todd's victim. He, or they, had settled the score.

Kim felt pleased with this line of deduction.

So how to trap him, or them?

By setting a trap! Brilliant! Set a trap, he, or they, fall in, they expose themselves. Case solved.

She cast her eyes over throng splashing in the lake. I'm going to trap you, whoever you are, she resolved.

"Listen" she said out loud. "I'm going to spin some stories, so you take note, but don't take anything I say literally. Got it?"

"Got it" was the reply.

And I play the damsel in distress once more, she determined.

*****

Now some people may consider it a complete chore, and a total waste of time, watching twenty nine towels being deployed vigorously over the twenty nine tanned, muscle bound frames of twenty nine super fit young men. But Kim was not one of those people. She considered the effort of propping herself up on one elbow to follow the proceedings with a close scrutiny well worth the trouble. A couple of photos snapped on her phone would secure the scene for the future. A short video would help too. Possibly a few more photos, and only a minute or two of extra video would suffice. And anyway, the background view was worth recording. The occasional glances of admiration cast in her direction were also appreciated.

Both the spectacle and her ruminations had put her in a jolly good mood. She was elated.

They drifted amiably down the hillside, to find the coach firmly stuck in the mire. The cautious driver had done his outright best to embed it there, and his sterling efforts had not gone unrewarded. Kim regarded this problem as being nothing whatsoever to do with herself, and decided her best course of action was to stand well back at a safe distance from the spray of black mud, and contribute to the effort by hurling a contrasting blend of encouragement, derision and insult to all those who entered into the fray of trying to haul or shove it out. Besides, watching this rather than participating was a splendid entertainment in its own right.

"Put your backs into it! Push! Shove it like you mean it! Pathetic! What a bunch of losers! I've seen more get up and go in a cactus! Feeble! That's it, it's shifting! Keep going! Useless!" and much more formed the outline of her bellowing.

Once freed from the clinging mud, the coach edged onto the road. The delighted troop invited Kim to board first, before stumbling on themselves.

Happy indeed were the souls carried down that mountain in the swerving and careering coach, as the driver sought to wrestle it around every gentle curve and fierce corner, aided only by brakes well lubricated with a slimy sticky morass of mire.

But even this joy was short lived, and the mud caked company alighted outside the hostel to seek showers and victuals.

*****

The evening meal consisted of roast chicken, accompanied by more roast chicken, and a mere splash of salad. Plenty of salad was on offer, there just weren't that many takers.

Kim addressed her companions.

"Great day in the mountains, wasn't it?" she began.

They all agreed.

"I feel so safe in the mountains, away from danger" she mused.

"Mountains are risky. Basically not safe at all" one ventured.

"But I feel safe, away from the threat in town" she replied.

"What threat?" another asked.

"Well, it's a long story. I don't want to put a downer on everyone" she dissembled.

"No, go on" insisted the first.

"Well, I have a friend, Rachel, who lives in Garda with her Italian boyfriend, Luciano. She always wears long sleeves, even when it's really hot. We tease her about it. Anyway, one time I went into the ladies, she was rinsing her face, and had taken her blouse off. I saw immediately that her arms and shoulders were covered in bruises, some new, some old" and she dramatically indicated her own arms.

"Shit, you don't say!" exclaimed one.

"So this boyfriend - Luciano - he batters her?" asked another.

"The only explanation" confirmed Kim.

"Bastard" they concluded.

"We've told her to leave him, loads of times, but she's too scared. He's so possessive. She's terrified of him" Kim enlarged.

"She should go to the police. That's a crime" volunteered another.

"We've tried to tell her, we have told her, over and over, but to no avail" Kim lied.

"So how come you end up in the mountains alone?" enquired another from the adjacent table.

"Well, it gets worse. A couple of weeks ago, Luciano made a pass at me. I told him where to go, in no uncertain terms" she reported emphatically.

"Good for you!" they responded.

"Next day, Rachel had a new, really big bruise. She said he hit her for no reason. Couple of days later, he made another pass at me. I told him to shove it. He never said a thing. Next day, Rachel had another bruised shoulder. She could hardly lift her arm" and Kim gestured to show the disability.

"Bastard" they repeated.

"Every time I say no, Rachel cops it. I didn't know what to do, so I just packed up and headed for the hills. Clear my mind. Think how to get out of this unholy mess" she added, and managed to produce a tear in her eye.

Her audience took up a lively discussion, and suggested she contact the police.

"Evidence?" asked Kim, pointing to her own arms "Not a mark on me, see?"

"Oh, he's clever isn't he? This Rachel won't complain, and you can't for lack of evidence. Cunning bastard" one surmised.

"Now you get it" claimed Kim.

This was quite enough, and she was sure the tale would be repeated around the group within twenty four hours.

The killer, or killers, would hear of a damsel in dire distress, and just might expose themselves by coming to her aid.

*****

The coach halted on the bridge over the ravine, simply because there was no where else it could stop. It completely blocked the bridge. Other traffic, which might come along at any time before dusk, it being a woodland road far from any habitat, would have to wait. The engine cut out, and the only sound was that of the rapids gushing below them.

"Right!" yelled Hank, standing up on the bus. "White water rafting! Everyone out of your kit, swimsuits on, sandals on. Cash, wallets, phones, watches, jewellery, teddy bears, anything else, stays on the bus. Driver will guard with his very life. Any questions? Right, let's get cracking!" and he showed them how.

Kim demurely followed suit at the rear of the bus. She switched off her precious phone, and abandoned it. I'm on my own now, she thought.

Hank led the way along the riverside as they heard the bus creak into life, and crawl away out of sight and hearing. They marched along briskly. Three tethered bright yellow inflatable rubber rafts came into sight on the bank, and three rows of wet suits and helmets. Paddles and life jackets were strewn around.

"Donatella here" and he pointed at her for those who were unsure, "will help you kit up correctly. If she can do it, then you can do it. Even an SLPS can do it" and he pointed to Kim for clarity.

The wet suits were clumsy and difficult to don; they assisted each other, Donatella helped Kim.

"You must be crazy girl, rafting with these ones" Donatella suggested.

"Crazier than you know" admitted Kim. "Thanks for the help".

Donatella now addressed the unruly mob.

"Five to a raft. First five, here please" and she indicated in the same way as Hank would have done. "Next five. Last five. Drag your raft to water edge, here," she pointed exactly where, "get in, hold tight, paddle to centre of current, hold on even tighter. Enjoy quick ride downstream. When you see blue sign on river bank, paddle over, get out, recover raft, carry back upstream along the riverside, not in the water. Easy".

Hank now had a turn. "Right. Usual safety rules. Arms and elbows in. No standing up to take selfies. No cameras anyway. Hold on for sheer bloody life. And no drowning without prior written permission from me".

The first five fairly raced towards their craft. They could hardly wait. In they piled in, squabbled for who could sit where, and wrestled each other for the paddles. The two victors manfully steered them into the centre current, and whoosh! They were away, barely visible in a torrent of white foam.

Oh my God, thought Kim. I'm next.

Donatella shoved her forward. In she climbed. She held on tight. She was graciously offered a paddle, she graciously declined. The gentle paddle into the centre flow was quite pleasant. There was an uneasy sensation of sliding down a slope in an uncontrolled way, followed by a visit to a watery hell. The coach rides had nothing on this. She was flung in so many directions in such a short time she became quite disoriented. She would have been launched out of the vessel altogether had not her companions clung onto her. It was later reported to her that her screams of terror were quite discernable above the roar of the rapids, and had echoed up and down the ravine, a vocal accomplishment to be envied.

The vessel slowed to a rush, and was skillfully steered towards the blue sign, a merciful beacon if ever there was one. They hauled the boat out, and Kim made some pretence of helping. She also pretended to help carry it back up, and was grateful to step aside when they told her she was getting in the way. The third raft stormed past them in a flurry of foam. They cheered it roundly.

Once they reached the starting point, Kim was happy to sit down, and recover her breath. The fifth group eagerly seized the vessel, and were quickly on their way.

As soon as the sixth group came back into sight, Kim braved a question.

"Hank, what time is the coach returning?"

"Just as soon as we've all completed our fifth and final run" was his immediate response.

"Oh, thanks" said Kim. Oh shit, she thought.

As her turn came around again, she grit her teeth and muttered to no one in particular "Once more into the breach, dear friend".

*****

When had she both completed and survived her final run, and staggered back up to the starting point, Kim pretty much just stood there while Donatella stripped her of her gear. She troubled herself to assist by raising an occasional limb, but only slightly. She flopped onto the sodden ground, and was just going to sprawl out when she spotted the coach. She was so pleased to see the coach parked on the bridge she yelled in delight.

"Look! The coach! The coach! It's come back for us!" and she leapt up with glee.

As soon as she was on the coach, she switched on her phone. It sparked into life, and once it had settled, she balled out "It's so good to be alive!"

This was met with a raucous cheer from her comrades.

She then managed to get dressed without any help from anyone. Quite a feat, she concluded.

*****

The evening meal was very welcome, and everybody sat there more or less in silence, devouring as much as possible as quickly as possible. Once refueled, and a few lagers later, a more merry mood ensued. Kim chatted amiably with her companions, as they each relived their experience of the day.

"Been there, seen it, done it, never again" assured Kim.

"You will, you know! Once a little time has passed, and it's been absorbed into your psyche, then given half a chance, you'll be back in the white water like a shot" a man named Harry insisted.

"Not me. Never again" Kim refuted.

"Bet you five Aussie dollars you do!" Harry wagered.

"And how the hell are going to enforce that wager, when you're back in Oz and the SLPS is stuck right here?" objected Sid.

"Fair point" accepted Harry.

"You're on!" cried Kim. "If I can go the next five years without even getting close to rapids, you have to pay up. I'll contact you via the facebook page".

"Now that's a bet! Bet accepted!" Harry confirmed.

"But she might cheat. Might go slinking down some rapids and you'd never know" suggested Sid.

"Hey, the only slinking I'll be doing is slinking in my bikini along a broad sunny beach, I can promise you that!" Kim riposted.

"Any chance of a preview?" hinted Harry, and they all laughed.

The conversation drifted along, and others joined and left the group, but no one raised the topic of the threat she had said she was under. Maybe no one's going to bite, she worried, and tomorrow was the last full day. She considered mentioning the subject herself, but thought it better to leave the story to stew, they all must have heard it by now.

So her mind flowed towards cheerier matters. The mood in the canteen was very upbeat, and all were having a good time. Thinking of good times, she thought she might quite like some more beneficence. In fact she would, she determined.

Her eyes flickered across the motley throng. And whom shall I enjoy tonight, she wondered. So lovely to have the choice. Her gaze alighted upon Tim. Such a nice boy. Well, Tim, it's your lucky night.

She deployed her very best come hither smile, bright, beaming, prolonged, piercing, unwavering, enthralling, enticing, irresistible.

Tim came hither. She repeated the same lurid lines as

previously; they had the same effect.

Once back in her room, she cleaned her teeth, brushed her hair, applied a thin smear of lipstick, loosened a button, switched off her phone, and sprayed perfume on her neckline.

At eleven o'clock sharp, taps rattled her door. She opened it, Tim was hauled in; he resisted her advances briefly, but he put up a sorry fight, he soon fell into her clutches, and she clutched supremely well.

She wrestled his clothes off him, then dragged her own garments off; he seemed to have little idea of the requisite procedure for the removal of feminine apparel.

He coarsely caressed her shoulder, she taught him a more tender place and a more delicate touch.

He shyly covered his member, she fiercely cast aside his feeble defence and boldly grasped; it responded promptly.

He appeared unsure of his next move, so she hurled him on the bed and pounced.

As he lay prostrate on his back, he knew further resistance was futile, and succumbed to her desire.

Straddling her prey so it could not wriggle free, she ripped open a condom with her teeth, roughly stretched the sheath over its trembling target, heaved herself into her favourite position, and set to work with a vengeance.

"Tim, Tim, Oh Tim!" she screeched aloud as a shattering orgasm seized the very fabric of her being.

"Whooaah!" he groaned as he climaxed, quite the same on both occasions.

Kim rolled off her quarry, and allowed the forlorn, exhausted creature to catch its breath.

"Oh, Tim, you were fabulous, absolutely fabulous! Thank you so much, that was terrific!" she exclaimed breathlessly.

"Fair dinkum" he replied.

She leapt upon him again, straddled him, and wrapping her hands around his throat, throttled him none too gently. He gasped and laughed at the same time. As she released her grip, he blurted "Bonzer, genuine belter!" and she relented, and lay back beside him.

Once she had recovered her composure, she whispered "You'd better go now" and he assembled his clothing, donned a minimum of attire, and escaped with barely a wave.

"What a lovely boy!" she spoke aloud, "nothing like a really nice lovely boy", and she then slipped into a delightful slumber.

8 THE LAST DAY

The whole group assembled in the common room. Three large display boards rested upon stout frames, and below each was a small table festooned with papers. Large maps were displayed on the boards, with red highlighted routes prominently shown.

"Right!" yelled Hank. "Last day! Hiking!" and he indicated the maps.

"Three routes, one map each" and he indicated with a long cane the three maps, so no one could have been uncertain.

"Route A is the hard one. Not for the faint hearted, to be sure. So think twice before you select that one" and he hit it with his stick.

That one's not for me, decided Kim.

He marched to the next board. "Route B is a damn sight harder, but here it is for those feeling a bit brave this morning" and he thumped the map which shook alarmingly.

He advanced upon the third. "Route C is a real bastard,

the bloody hardest of them all, so only total drongoes need apply" and he stabbed at the map with his cane.

"So pick your poison, and have a great day. Check your phone's GPS is on. Get the app of your route and its local map from the link on the display board, and download it to your phone. No excuses. Pick up a paper map from the pile on the table. Pick up a compass, put it round your neck. Two ways to navigate, no excuses. Got it? So who's for Route A? Queue here" and he pointed to the floor in front of display A.

Kim timidly stepped forward and queued alone.

"Queue here for Route B" and he pointed to the floor in front of display B.

A mob surged forward.

"Queue here for Route C" and he pointed to the floor in front of display C, for clarity.

The rest lined up.

Three defected from Route B to Route A.

Kim turned, and whispered "Thanks guys".

Everyone picked up maps, compasses, and fiddled with their phones.

"All set? Back for dinner, not back by nightfall, search parties and a black eye from the Mountain Rescue. Got it? Get cracking!" and Hank joined group C.

Kim and her companions set off at a moderate pace, and it was not long before the other two groups were out of sight.

"I'm Kim" she said.

“We know” they all answered.

“Simon” said one.

“Andy” said another.

“Beamer” said the third.

“What was your mother thinking?” quipped Kim.

“Not my real name. Just got a beaming smile”, and he demonstrated it.

“Lucky they don’t call you Dracula, it’s more like the grimace of a vampire” she riposted.

They chuckled, and as they hiked on, they all chatted further, and she grew to enjoy their company.

The sun rose higher in the sky, it got hotter, and after a long steady climb Kim wanted a little rest. They stopped for a packed lunch and a refreshing drink. Their rest extended somewhat, and a shorter route was resolved upon unanimously.

They ambled freely over the high ground, and revelled in the serene beauty of the landscape, taking in the wonderful views around them. Kim spotted a snake of figures windings its way up a distant hillside.

“Route C” ventured Simon.

“Probably” replied Kim.

“Dead cert” said Andy.

The afternoon wore on, and the circular path they had followed brought the sight of the hostel into view far below them.

"We could sit here a bit" suggested Beamer.

"Sound one" agreed Andy, and they all flopped down onto the warm grass.

Kim lay back and let the sunbeams gently caress her face.

"You seem happy up here in the hills" observed Simon.

"I am. So peaceful. So relaxing. So free of the stresses and strains of modern life" she responded.

"Yeah, well we heard a bit about your troubles back in town" fished Andy.

"You did?" Kim sounded surprised. "That was nothing, really" she added vaguely.

"Didn't sound like nothing. Sounded like a whole load of shit" Beamer hinted.

"Well" began Kim, and she repeated the whole fabrication directly for their benefit. Lurid details were added, and fresh embellishments were introduced.

They listened attentively and sympathetically.

"Sometimes, Rachel says that she wishes he were dead, gone from her life forever" she completed her tale.

The three glanced at each other; a silent assent was exchanged.

"Now today may just be your lucky day. I'm Simon, Equalizer" he said.

"Andy, Equalizer" admitted Andy.

"Beamer, Equalizer" chimed Beamer.

"Meet The Three Equalizers" Simon grandly said. "We put right what others cannot, or will not".

"We dispense a higher justice, what we call Deep Justice" Andy pronounced darkly.

"One that's effective permanently" explained Beamer.

"I don't quite follow" Kim uttered.

"You see" began Simon, "it all started years ago. I live in a pretty little town, almost in the outback. I had a little cousin, a boy of twelve. Didn't know him that well, didn't really like him, he was a scrawny, cheeky little bugger. Much younger than me, I hardly knew him really. But he was my cousin. He was a human being. He did have a right to life. Some drunk driver flattened him, left him for dead. He was dead. They caught the shit, a drunk van driver. He got jail time. But he only actually served about eighteen months, then he was back out in our little town again, as large as life. Banned from driving for life. That's not justice. Then I saw him drinking again, he hadn't learnt a thing. Then he vanished. So, I thought, where's he gone? Adelaide is the nearest city, so I went there, checked out recent ads for van drivers, waited outside the premises of the various businesses who'd advertised. Finally saw the shit, driving a van. Must have got a false identity. Thought I'd call the cops, but nah, they won't do shit. Went home. Turned it over in my mind. Went back to Adelaide, saw him drinking and driving at the same time, with my own eyes. Resolved there and then I was going to work a number on him. No way he's gonna flatten another kid".

"Oh my God, that's shocking" mumbled Kim.

"Then there was my granny, nice old lady" Beamer began. "A widow, but reasonably well off. She met some old duffer at a country dance class, seemed a decent enough bloke. They dated for a while, and then he moved in. Met him a couple of times, chatty old geezer, and she seemed happy with him. Didn't think much about it. Then he vanished, left her a bouquet of flowers".

"Nice touch, I suppose" said Kim.

"She was sad" continued Beamer, "for a while. Went shopping, card declined - insufficient funds".

"Oh no!" cried Kim.

"Oh yes!" bellowed Beamer. "Account cleared out, savings withdrawn - vanished in fact, credit cards maxed out, personal loans taken out against her pension, loan against her car, new mortgage on her house. She was totally broke, beyond broke, in deep financial shit. Family had to shell out just to feed her".

"That is horrific! What did the police do?" demanded Kim.

"Precious little. Said it was a crime mitigated by contributory negligence. They did shit nothing" Beamer spat out the words.

"So what happened next?" Kim enquired.

"I tracked the blighter down. Neighbours opposite had a CCTV, and we got the car reg off it. Mate of a mate got the address. I went there. Bloody enormous mansion, huge grounds, range of elegant outbuildings, Rolls and a Merc in the driveway, terraced gardens reaching down to the river, boathouse and boat. Saw the old man himself in his garden, happily pruning his roses. Nearly strangled him there and then. Must have fleeced a dozen old dears to amass a fortune like that. Thought I'd get some cash off him, pay my gran back. Couple of weeks later, she died of a heart attack. All that stress and strain. I said right. That man is a dead man".

"I get it, I really do" Kim muttered.

"My sister is a sweet little sister. We argue often and bitterly, but that's our prerogative as siblings" explained Andy. "At college, this guy raped her. Her word against his. He got away with it. Or so he thought. My sister asked around. Two other girls said the same, but wouldn't formally come forward. He'd got away with them too. Three bloody rapes. Or so he thought".

"Oh my God!" repeated Kim.

"Now one fine day, we three pitiful buggers met, and chatted, and exchanged woes, and resolved to act together. The Three Equalizers were born" Simon announced.

"Totally get that!" Kim exclaimed.

"You see, it's not that these shits had done something wrong. It's deliberate, repeated wrongs, going unpunished. They're not gonna stop, 'til someone stops them" Andy said through gritted teeth.

"We dispense Deep Justice where and when it's needed" boasted Beamer.

"So what did you do, about these three villains?" Kim enquired anxiously.

"Well, that greedy old man, he suffered an unfortunate hit and run accident. He did not survive" Beamer stated.

"Now as for that van driver. Bit more complicated. Andy met him in a bar one fine night, got him really drunk" Simon explained.

"Not a difficult task" Andy chipped in.

Simon continued. "Then he loaded him in his own van, drove out of town to where there's a flyover, and some nice thick massive concrete pillars. Meanwhile we two borrowed a power winch from the gliding club, really powerful, gets those gliders shifting fast, you know the sort of thing".

Kim nodded she understood.

"Then we wrapped a spare cable right around the pillar, and attached both ends to the van. Hooked the winch cable to that one, and hey presto, the van with engine running, shithead in the driving seat, accelerated up to high speed and wham! Straight into the concrete he went!" and Simon ended his soliloquy with a loud clap of his hands.

"Deep Justice" intoned Beamer.

"Police identified him of course, totally believed the obvious. Never spotted that we couldn't extricate the two cable ends from the wreckage, had to cut the cable away, and leave two bits behind" Simon proudly announced.

"Now this rapist" started Andy, "damn sight harder. Lived in a tiny town in the Northern Territory. Couldn't just arrive and do him in. So we had to wait. We got his address, and posted him offers, and competitions, and so on, seemingly from real companies. He never replied. But finally, one competition caught his fancy. He applied, filled in his email address, and returned the form. Once we had that, we got a mate to crack it open, get the password. Took him bloody weeks. But he got it for us. Then we read his emails. Watched and waited. Saw him book a holiday in Italy. So we booked it too!"

"Brilliant!" enthused Kim. "Go on!"

Andy went on. "We planned the whole thing, down to the last detail. Chose the place and time. Befriended him on the plane. Got bikes from the hostel bike store, there round the back" and he pointed to it for Kim's benefit "and in the middle of the night we all went cycling to this sleepy little place with an old castle. Slipped a mickey finn in his drink - actually a bit of Aussie snake venom - and finished him off below the castle walls".

"My God!" cried Kim. "The guy whose holiday I'm on right now!"

"Yup" Andy confirmed.

"He got his head bashed in. Staged it so it looked like a fall, placed climbing gear around. Nice bit of stage craft, if you ask me" added Beamer.

"And he'd stuck a little something in my sister, so I stuck a little something in his heart" snarled Andy.

"Whole set up fooled the Italian police. They still think it was an unlucky accident. Real bozos" Beamer boasted.

"Yes they are!" agreed Kim. "Especially the Carabinieri. They're right dozy gits!"

"So this Luciano bloke. He's a repeat offender, right?" Simon asked.

"Continually" confirmed Kim.

"And he's not gonna stop, and right now, no one's stopping him" added Andy.

"And even if your Rachel did leave him, and got away in one piece, he'd latch onto some other poor sheila and make her life hell. He's never gonna stop" Beamer argued.

"But we can stop him. Stop him guaranteed" promised Simon.

"That's what's needed, right?" asked Andy.

"Yes, it is" agreed Kim.

"Okay then. We'll work a number on him" Simon darkly pronounced.

"So it's Luciano, right?" queried Beamer.

"Luciano Benetti, Strada Condetti, thirty six, Garda" Kim advised.

"His home? Tricky. Where's he work?" Simon asked.

"Not sure, it's a bakery in Garda, let me check, I'll know it when I see the name" Kim replied vaguely.

She fiddled with her phone. The screen glowed 'Forno Ambrosio, Corsia Nuova' which she read aloud.

Simon browsed on his phone. "Got it. Easy!" he cried.

"He works on the night shift, starts at midnight" Kim added helpfully.

"What car's he drive?" Andy asked.

"Not sure. Got a picture of Rachel, though, and I'm sure the car's in the background" Kim answered, and she pretended to flip through her gallery of photos. The screen glowed and faded once more. 'Green Fiat Punto, EP 261582' and she related the details.

"Right then. All set" Simon declared.

"So what will you do?" Kim enquired.

"Need to know basis. And you don't need to know" Beamer answered.

"Let's just say he'll have a nasty accident, and by the time his body is found, we'll all be back in Oz" Simon stated.

"Yeah, it's our last day in Italy" Andy said.

"Luciano's too" added Beamer.

They chuckled with a sinister overtone.

"Let's get back down now", Simon suggested, and glancing at Kim, "we'll speak of this no more".

"Think I'll stay up here a while longer. Take in the view. Clear my head" Kim replied.

"Fine. Then we'll say farewell, fair maiden Kim" Andy said, and he reached to shake her hand.

Each of them shook her hand.

"We won't speak to you again, so this really is farewell" Simon said, and the three began their descent.

"Good luck, keep safe" yelled Kim before they were out of earshot.

Once they were a good two hundred yards away, and fifty feet or more lower, Kim asked aloud "You get all that?"

Her screen glowed. 'Yes, got it all'.

Moments later it glowed again 'Well done. CSA".

"Will Luciano and Rachel be safe?" Kim sought assurance.

'Perfectly. Already under protection. CSA' was the response.

The screen glowed again. 'Is this Andy?' and a photo appeared.

"Yes" said Kim.

'Is this Simon?' another photo was presented.

"Yes" she confirmed.

'Is this Beamer?'

"No" she denied.

'Is this Beamer' a different individual was offered.

"No, that's Bodger" corrected Kim.

'Is this Beamer?'

"Yes" she said. The screen fell dark.

Kim rested in silence, watching the figures below her trudging to their doom. Half of her wanted to run after them, give them a warning, but it was far too late for that. They were triple killers, even though she completely understood and sympathized with their motives.

After an hour, they had vanished from sight, and Kim slowly made her own way down to the hostel.

*****

The whole throng gathered in the canteen, and ate as if they had not been fed for days. Drinks were distributed, and gratefully quaffed, when Hank arose one final time to address his audience.

"Right you are then! Home tomorrow! Last night in this tidy little palace!"

A loud roar greeted this announcement, whether of approval or dissent it was hard to tell.

"So everybody had a great time?"

A definitely positive roar was bellowed.

"Got off to a sticky start, but someone came and saved the day".

Another roar.

"So now I've got to award our final certificate. Man of the Mountains. There are two possible candidates, there's me, and there's the SLPS" Hank explained.

"You decide. Now there's me, expert in all matters outdoors, your fearless leader, truly wise, and great fun to boot. Then there's the SLPS, found dangling on a rope half way up a cliff not knowing where her arse is from now until next Christmas."

"So let's hear it for me!"

Loud booing ensued.

"Let's hear it for the SLPS!"

Loud cheering followed.

"The SLPS has it! Come on up!" Hank directed.

Kim came forward, and gratefully accepted her accolade.

Emblazoned in large letters it read:-

'MAN OF THE MOUNTAINS'
'SKINNY LITTLE POMMY SHEILA'

Kim laughed, and held it up for all to see. She curtseyed

profusely to load applause.

They all reverted to a babble of discourse, going over the highlights of the trip. Kim returned to her seat, and joined in the conversation animatedly, but she did notice one trio quietly slope away.

Their fate is now sealed, she sighed to herself.

*****

9 EXTRACTION

In the morning, a rapid breakfast was followed by clearing and packing, and the heavy packs were hauled onto the bus. The whole group assembled in the sunshine. Hank was not happy. A quick role call established three were missing.

"Right!" he yelled. "We'll pack their bags for them!" and he organized this, and it was soon done. A search was conducted; three bikes were missing. Consternation was evident all round.

There was no sign of the three. A police car arrived, and the policemen got out, and spoke to the Italian hosts. The three packs were identified, and were loaded into the police car, which drove away. No explanation was offered.

"Right!" yelled Hank. "Off we go then, three men down, evidently in the dutiful care of the local rozzers. Outside my brief, so away we go!"

Kim watched all these proceedings silently.

Each one of them came to say goodbye, and shook her hand. Mike and Tim ventured a kiss on her cheek. She smiled graciously. Finally Hank came, shook her hand wholeheartedly, and quietly said "Bye Kim".

The bus crawled away down the lane, crunching its gears and leaving a trail of smoky haze in its wake.

Kim watched it until it fell from sight, when a tear welled in her eye. She wiped it away. Her phone beeped. She looked at it. Text message. She opened the text.

'Surveillance ended'

So now she really was alone, and wept openly.

She waited for a long time, all of seven minutes in fact, standing entirely alone in front of the deserted hostel.

A taxi crept into sight, and pulled up in front of her.

"Tomlinson?" enquired the driver.

"Yes" she managed, and she climbed in, while he loaded her packs.

The return journey was uneventful. She enjoyed the comfort and quiet of the ride, but felt intensely lonely. She'd never see any of them again, and had not realized just how attached to them she'd become. Tears flowed freely. Thirty holidaymakers. One girl, two lovers, three killers, and twenty four really great guys.

*****

The taxi pulled into the familiar driveway of the Commissario. She reluctantly dragged herself out, leaving her bags to the driver.

The front door swung open, revealing the Commissario's beaming smile. He ran forward, swept her into his arms, lifted her up like a rag doll, and gave her a huge bear hug. He finished off the welcome with a tiny peck on her cheek.

"Come in, come in!" he invited, waving her inside.

She recovered her breath, and tip toed into the hall.

"I'll get your packs" he insisted, and seized them, dumping them in the front room. Her own bag was still in the same place.

"Come on in, sit down" he cried, and she followed him into the rear room as before. It looked exactly the same.

They sat down.

"Are Luciano and Rachel okay?" Kim enquired.

"Totally safe" assured the policeman. "They have no idea of the part they played, entirely safe".

"And the culprits? Are they still in one piece?" Kim demanded to know.

"Of course! Safely under lock and key. No problem at all" he responded. "But what about you? You look very well, are you very well?"

"I'm just dandy. Tell me what happened" she instructed.

"We took Luciano's car. He was then impersonated by one of our men, ex special forces, very skilled. He wore a steel baseball cap, and had reasonable body armour beneath his jacket. We tracked the three all the way to Garda, and right to the bakery, where they lay in wait for their intended victim. We had prepositioned men around, so our trap enclosed their trap" and his arms made a grand circular gesture.

"Go on" said Kim.

"The car pulled up, he got out, they immediately advanced, he whirled around and disarmed one of them, our officers charged out, tasers at the ready, yelling 'Polizia' like crazy. It was fun to watch. They saw the six officers, squad cars screeching round the corner, and gave up. Pity. My men were hoping for some real action".

"At least they weren't hurt," Kim said "they weren't really evil villains".

"Bad enough, I think. They had to be stopped".

"So what happens to them now?" she enquired.

"They were separated and questioned immediately. They each admitted everything" he answered.

"So what next?" Kim insisted.

"As Australians, and all their victims were Australians, and the first two killings were in Australia, they face justice there".

"What about the assault on Luciano?" Kim asked.

"We forget it. It was entrapment anyway. We're happy to let the Australians deal with their own. Six marshalls are on their way to Roma. They will go home under guard. Our involvement over" and he smiled, and waved his hands in the air.

"But they did have understandable motives. What do you think of their Deep Justice?" Kim enquired.

"Look, two kinds of justice. Private and public. A thousand and more years ago justice was a private matter. Someone wronged you, you hit back yourself, or your family did. It always ended the same, killings and more killings. Vengeance, feuds, vendettas, never ending, as retaliation followed retaliation. Public justice has independent investigation" and he pointed to himself, "open courts where evidence is provided and challenged, and an impartial judge to meet out a fair punishment. Public justice is imperfect, private justice is an absolute disaster".

"I suppose so" said Kim.

"And remember, those three were on their way to kill a perfectly innocent man, based solely on your say so. No investigation of the facts, they didn't even confirm your story with Rachel".

"Could have been true for all you know" Kim objected.

"I sent someone round to deliver a parcel, which was actually misaddressed, to see Rachel. She answered the door, and was wearing a sleeveless top. No bruises visible. So we, the Carabinieri, know for a fact that your fabrication was a fabrication. Just to be sure".

"Sneaky. Do I have to fill in any forms?" Kim hopefully enquired.

"Not at all. You weren't involved in either the investigation or the arrest, no part to play whatsoever, so no forms" and he grinned innocently.

She got up and kicked him; he laughed long and loudly.

"Well, now we're on kicking terms, you may call me Francesco. Anyway, no forms, definitely no forms. A little unofficial assistance, maybe, I grant you that" and he laughed again.

Kim smiled at last.

"So, Francesco, I'm glad it's all over now" she stated.

"Well, not quite" he contradicted. "I have here a

certificate, appointing me as an official spokesman for the Ministry of Justice, for one week only" and he waved the document at her.

"Well bully for you!" she snapped.

"Thank you kindly for your most gracious compliment" and he bowed his head solemnly.

"I meant every word of it" she riposted.

"So in my capacity of official spokesman, I thank you on behalf of the Ministry of Justice" and he waved his paper.

"Thank you" Kim intoned modestly.

He put his police hat on. "And speaking for the Carabinieri, our total gratitude, we could not have solved this intractable case without you".

Kim accepted his thanks. "You're welcome".

He removed his hat and picked up his document again, raising it aloft, and took a deep breath. "So the Ministry of Justice enquires if you had sex with any of the boys in the hostel?"

Kim blushed scarlet. "Of course not! What kind of girl do you take me for?"

He lowered the paper, and put his police hat on again. "I did tell you that we would be listening twenty four seven. When you switched your phone off, that only muted the speaker, and blanked the screen. The surveillance function still continued all the time".

Kim thought about what this meant, realized what it meant, blushed a deep vermillion, and covered her face.

"Oh my God! You heard everything! You must think I'm a

right slag!" and she cried so much she shuddered and shook. Tears streamed down her face, and wetted her hands.

"Please, please, don't be upset, not at all. Be assured, no one judges you. You were a young woman in a dangerous place, and no one can blame you. So be tranquil, be tranquil" and he wrapped his arms around her and held her tight.

She calmed down a little.

"You must despise me" she wailed.

"Not one bit. You are a young woman, with a healthy appetite for life. And so it should be. Sex is a part of life, it's a good thing to have in your life, so be tranquil, please" he reassured her.

"You must think I'm a right slag" she repeated quietly.

"No. Not at all. It's a well-known fact that when people are in danger, it raises their senses and heightens their appetites. They talk a lot, drink a lot, eat a lot, and love a lot. It's quite natural. It's healthy. Not a bad thing at all".

"I suppose" she muttered.

He waved his paper aloft once more. "But, I have to tell you, that some of the officers monitoring you, were young men, and young men can do silly things".

This sounds ominous thought Kim. "Like what?"

"They isolated those portions of the sound track where you made your assignations, and completed your assignations, and then shared them among friends".

Kim had to think what this implied. "You are joking?"

"Alas not. Those friends shared with others, uploaded to websites, and so on".

Kim stared at him aghast. "You mean.....?"

"I'm afraid so. The adventures of Mike and Tim are very popular. So far there's been over eleven thousand hits" he informed in a matter of fact tone. "Many more every hour" he added helpfully. "No chance now of recalling the sound track from the Internet at large".

Kim was speechless for once.

He put on his police hat. "As a senior officer, I apologize sincerely on behalf of the Carabinieri, and can assure you that disciplinary proceedings have been held, and the officers involved reprimanded, they have been fined, and a note entered into their records. It will impact on their promotion prospects".

Kim was unimpressed.

He took his hat off, and waved his document high.

"The Ministry of Justice apologizes unreservedly, admits its guilt in breaching your privacy under the General Data Protection Regulations, and invites you to waive your right to seek damages in open court by signing this affidavit" and he pushed another document towards her, "and accepting as compensation this twenty five thousand Euros in cash" and he pulled out a holdall and showed her the money.

Kim stared at it. She stared at him. She stared at the document.

"Look, I'm so sorry about this" and tears welled in his eyes now, "after all you've been through, and done for us, it really is shocking, and I apologize personally, I never saw it coming, I would have prevented it, but it's done, and can't be undone. If you go to open court, there will be huge publicity, the tracks will become infamous, you'll never be rid of it. Sign, we all forget about it. The idiots out there on the Internet will soon enough find some other silly diversion" and he offered her the pen.

She signed and dated. She grabbed the bag. "Mine, I think" she said coldly.

"Absolutely" he confirmed. "Ready for a latte, now?" and he smiled sweetly.

She kicked him again. "Yes. And hurry up with it, Francesco" and kicked him once more as he went off chuckling merrily.

*****

Once they had made peace, and after a rather modest lunch, it was time for Kim to go. A lift was taking her away at two o'clock sharp.

"So, my little secret agent" said the Commissario, "you had better collect all your things".

He led her into the front room, and left her alone to change into her own clothing. It was great to be back in her own clothes again. He returned shortly.

"The camping and climbing stuff, we can put here, for return to the rescue team" and he sorted and shifted it. "All the garments they provided are yours to keep now, they don't want them back".

"Wonderful" said Kim, holding aloft the climbing boots. "These will match my pretty pink summer dress so nicely" and she flung them at him.

He ducked very adeptly considering his size, then tripped on the boots he was laughing so much. He fell onto the camping pack and rolled onto the floor.

"Help me up, wonder woman" he pleaded.

"Not on your nelly" she remarked. "And you can sort out your own mess next time".

A car swerved into the driveway, horn blaring.

"Your lift is here, I believe" he blurted out.

"At last" said Kim. "I've had enough of you for this month, thank you".

"Maybe I can see you next month, take you out to dinner?" he asked politely.

"Maybe, maybe not. We'll see" she primly riposted. Sounds good to me, she thought, can't wait. Only a couple of days to next month anyway.

He opened the front door, and loaded the luggage, including the holdall, into the boot of the Alfa Romeo. Kim peered at the driver.

"Svetlana!" and she quickly climbed in. She barely managed a goodbye wave as the car sped off. She just about made out an 'Arrivederci' on his lips before he was out of sight.

"My little heroine!" began Svetlana. "I know the outline, it must have been horrific stuck in a horrid hostel with nothing but mountain men for days on end".

"It was a challenge" admitted Kim, "especially the rancid stench of all that male sweat".

"Ugh! It sounds disgusting!" and Svetlana grimaced.

"Was a bit" said Kim.

"And I suppose a few of them tried to have sex with you?" Svetlana fished.

"A few did, and a few failed, that's for sure" Kim responded. No need to mention the two who succeeded, she mused.

"You poor girl" Svetlana sympathized.

"It's so good to see a pretty face, I mean a familiar face" Kim remarked.

"Thank you. I prefer pretty to familiar, so I'll take that as a compliment. Of course I prefer beautiful to pretty, and absolutely gorgeous really. First compliment of the day. So nice to have someone say I'm absolutely gorgeous" Svetlana smirked.

Kim laughed. "My God, I've missed you! Missed you so much!"

"Of course you have. I missed you too. I will take you out for a really nice dinner, when you're ready".

"Deal" promised Kim.

"And I must say you're looking very tanned, and really trim and fit. Very sexy" Svetlana ventured.

"Thanks. I am fit, and I think I've lost a couple of pounds too" Kim replied. "But back to work tomorrow, I suppose".

"No, no, you take a couple of days off. We have the roster covered. I've enjoyed the change anyway" Svetlana assured her.

"Thanks, I was hoping for that" Kim admitted.

"And your suite is ready and waiting for you" Svetlana said.

"Thank God! Can't wait for a hot bath and my own comfortable bed. And some decent food. Beans and chips for days on end is a nightmare in itself" Kim lamented.

"You poor girl!" Svetlana repeated.

The car sped along the highways with abandon, and Garda soon came into view. It swerved into the hotel car park sending gravel flying, and halted with a jolt. The porter kindly carried her bags and packs inside, but she was careful to carry the holdall herself.

"Ciao!" called Svetlana accompanied by a chorus of tinkling gravel.

Once she was settled back in her room, and had had a delicious hot bath, Kim lay on her bed, and sighed. So many nice boys. Should have had the lot, not just two.

10 AFTERMATH

The weekly meeting started in a desultory fashion, and continued at an ever slowing pace. It had been some days now since Kim had returned to her normal duties, which she had enjoyed at first, but a tinge of boredom was creeping in. Listening to Sara drone on about schedules fanned that boredom to a doze.

"So Kim, what do you think?" Sara demanded to know in a loud clear voice.

Kim sat up with an exaggerated cough, and cleared her throat.

"So, you don't agree then?" Sara asked.

"Well, not really" Kim ventured.

"So no thousand Euro bonus for you then, I take it. Moving on" Sara shuffled her papers.

The other three laughed at her.

"Dozy git. Obvious you weren't paying attention" Griff said.

"You poor sod. If only you'd been listening. And we'd all have been witnesses to the offer!" Alice retorted.

"Never mind. We've all dozed off in meetings too. We missed our grand bonus once in just the same way" Rachel smiled at her.

"So how was Verona, Kim?" Sara asked.

"Okay, Went back and forth, like you said. No problems" she lied freely.

"Fine" Sara replied.

Sara had some more droning to do, so she did it.

"Meeting over!" she suddenly cried.

"Yey!" yelped Kim, far too loudly. "I mean, thanks, Sara, for an informative meeting".

"Don't push it" she replied.

"Hey, Kim, here's a conundrum for you. My boyfriend, Luciano, went out one evening to go to work, and his car was gone" Rachel said.

"Oh, no!" they all responded.

"So he called the local police, and they said come to the station, so he did, they asked for proof of ID, so he returned to get that, went back to the station, and they asked for his car documents, which he had. Then they couldn't find the right form. Can you believe it?" she asked.

"I can" said Kim.

"Anyway, eventually, they found it, filled it all in, pages and pages of it, and were kind enough to run him to work. And guess what?" Rachel asked.

"What?" they duly replied.

"His car was right there, where he usually parks it at work" she stated.

"The policeman says 'is that your car?' he says 'well yes' so the copper says stop wasting police time and clears off" and Rachel raised her hands in astonishment.

"Was it damaged?" queried Sara.

"Not one bit. In fact it had been cleaned and polished, tidied and vacuumed inside, and had a full tank of petrol. So can you explain that, Kim?" Rachel challenged.

They all keenly awaited her response.

"Well" said Kim, "I think some guy had the documents for a written off car, the same make and model as his".

"Green Fiat Punto" Rachel offered.

"Right. And then this guy offers such a car for sale, but doesn't actually steal it until he has a buyer lined up. He spots Luciano's car, and watches it, where it's parked and so on. Then when he gets a buyer, he steals the car, cleans it all up, fills up, and takes it straight to the buyer, with the new car ID. But the buyer backs out, for some reason, so now the thief has a hot car, with nowhere to hide it, so he just returns it, leaves it where it should be. Everybody's happy, no drama, police don't care, and the thief survives to steal another day".

They all seem convinced by this explanation.

"So if he finds another buyer, he'll be back to steal it again?" Rachel worried.

"Get an alarm and a steering wheel lock. He'll look for easier pickings elsewhere" Kim suggested.

"We'll do that" promised Rachel, "and thanks".

Nice story, thought Kim. More believable than the truth.

*****

Kim was slumped on her bed just wondering what to order for dinner. The phone interrupted her decision making process.

"Hi" she said.

"Miss Tomlinson? Lord Tomlinson's secretary. He can fit you in at Bergamo tomorrow evening. Is that convenient?"

"Yes, super" replied Kim.

"Excellent. Car will pick you up at six, if that's alright?"

"Six is fine" she confirmed.

"Goodbye" and the line went dead.

Okay. That's tomorrow's dinner sorted. Now back to tonight's.

*****

The Bentley glided silently into the car park. The chauffeur got out and opened a door for her. So nice to be looked after like a lady.

The car cruised swiftly along the autostrada, and headed for a hotel near Bergamo airport.

She was welcomed at the door, and taken into the dining

room, where Lord Tomkinson sat chatting on his phone. He ended his call, and rose to greet her.

"Kim, lovely to see you again, do take a seat" he greeted her, and kissed her on the cheek.

"Thanks, good to see you too, daddy" she said.

He laughed. "And to your good fortune" and he raised his glass.

"Which reminds me, daddy" she said, "you quite forgot my birthday present and my Christmas present".

He laughed again. "Hey, I'm not that sort of a daddy, I'm not a sugar daddy".

Now Kim laughed. "No, never that" she added.

They ordered drinks, and looked at the menu, and selected their meals.

After they had eaten, Lord Tomlinson renewed the conversation.

"So, Kim, how's your life been, anything different to report?"

"Oh, you know, same old, same old" she responded.

"Right, good. Must have been the other daughter then, my real one" he replied.

"What must have been?" enquired Kim.

"Well, the Australian High Commissioner contacted me, and invited me to luncheon" he said.

"Is he a friend of yours?" Kim asked.

"Never met him before" he answered, "but along I went, and he told me he wanted to thank me personally for the service wrought by my daughter in bringing to justice, three killers, who between them had slain three Australian victims, two in Australia, and one in Italy. So if it wasn't you, it must have been my other daughter. She must have nipped out of her bank in Frankfurt, popped over to Italy, solved the case, and hopped back to work next day. And there was I thinking she is as dull as dishwater".

Kim laughed. "Oh that caper, yes there was that. You're quite right of course, 'twas I who wielded the sword of justice".

"Never doubted it, my dear, never doubted it. You do lead an interesting life, don't you?" he claimed.

"Yes, I do" she admitted, and proceeded to tell him the whole tale, omitting no humiliation, exhilaration or assignation, and he relished the whole and laughed merrily.

THE END

Printed in Great Britain
by Amazon